D1168561

19.95

Bitterroot
Landing

Bitterroot Landing

SHERI REYNOLDS

G. P. PUTNAM'S SONS
New York

*This is a work of fiction. The events
and characters portrayed are imaginary.
Their resemblance, if any, to real-life
counterparts is entirely coincidental.*

G. P. Putnam's Sons
Publishers Since 1838
200 Madison Avenue
New York, NY 10016

Library of Congress Cataloging-in-Publication Data

Reynolds, Sheri.
Bitterroot Landing / Sheri Reynolds.
p.   cm.
ISBN 0-399-13994-X (alk. paper)
1. Young women—Southern States—Fiction.   I. Title.
PS3568.E8975B58   1994   94-4915 CIP
813'.54—dc20

Printed in the United States of America
1   2   3   4   5   6   7   8   9   10

This book is printed on acid-free paper.

ACKNOWLEDGMENTS

With thanks to my readers: Laura Gabel Hartman,
Magghi Tinsley, Joy Humphrey, Mary Lou Hall,
Kwadwo Agymah Kamau, Glen Turner, Sandra
McKinnon, Roland Dierauf, Mary Louise Taylor,
Erica Hector, and especially Tom De Haven.

For Ruth, Libby, and Gail

Part One

For as long as I can remember, I've searched for things to worship—bits of rock, storm fronts, bugs with turquoise glitter on their wings. But rocks chip, storms churn themselves out, and bugs can be crushed with a heel or a raindrop. Gods change colors and spin themselves new garments every day. The most we can hope for is to be allowed to watch.

I have learned that the products of worship are always two-fold. If you study the moon too hard for too long, it will fall down luminous upon you. And with moon in your eyes and moon anchoring your feet, you can never see the stars again.

I'm looking for the place where worship finds balance, where it does not debase me or exalt me so high that I can't return. Gods change colors and spin themselves new garments every day. I want to be able to stand in awe of them, one at a time.

When I was a child, I swung on a vine in the woods behind my Mammie's house. Thin-barked and flexible, the vine bounced beneath my weight. In winter while the snakes slept, I claimed that vine, named it, loved it naked, leafless for me. I was skinny with arms like a boy's, and I could scale the vine up, up into the trees, throwing pinecones at scrawny yard chickens that scratched below.

In spring I had to share with other creatures. Because I was afraid of snakes, I carried a heavy stick to beat them. Each new bloom of leaves got in my way, and so I plucked them off, every one, to keep them from cluttering my space. I'd strip whole branches with one hand while clutching my vine with the other, only stopping when I noticed that beneath the dirt, the only part of my palms that didn't bleed were the calluses.

On stormy evenings, my Mammie would scratch my back and tell me stories about wild animals that could talk even better than people, her breath scented with the bloody maple of coughs. I'd seen her talk the fire out of burns and whisper secrets to warts that made them drop right off my knees, so I believed her. Mammie was ancient, red and wrinkled, smelling of dirt and old papers, and I could see strips of her head beneath the strands of hair that pulled back to form a tiny dark fist at her neck.

In the summer when green plants sprouted from dark garden soil, Mammie sat on an overturned foottub between the rows, nursing each leaf.

"This here," she'd say, "this here'll make you sleepy. Taste."

"It's a *weed,*" I'd protest. "I don't want to go to sleep."

"Open your mouth," she'd say. " 'Tain't no weed." And she'd place the leaf on my tongue, watching until I swallowed. Then she'd whisper the plant names to me again and again. Liverwort. Bitterroot. Blessed thistle.

Mammie knew a lot for an old woman. Afternoons when we did my lessons, she made me practice both alphabets—the one I learned in school and the one she used to read her special books.

Each morning she'd walk me down the dirt trail to the road where the bus stopped, pointing out patterns in spiderwebs or secrets she heard from the clouds. "Don't you tell 'em the things I teach you," she'd say. "School's another kind of learnin'."

"I won't tell," I'd promise, and she'd slap me hard across the face—as a warning, she said.

At school I listened but didn't speak unless I was called on. The teacher moved me into a class with older children who stared at me and whispered when I answered the questions they could not. One boy called me names until, finally, I spit on his shoe. A girl cried out, "It's a curse," and he backed away, his eyes round as half-dollar pieces. After that, they left me alone.

For miles around, people knew about Mammie's secret wisdom. They knew she had special ways to brew her drinks that made them the sweetest and strongest around. But they didn't know the *real* secret. I'd seen Mammie mold great pitchers out of clay she dug from the ground, talking to the stiff red mud all the time she shaped it with her knotty hands. And after she had burned the clay hard, she poured her liquor into the pitchers and left it there to absorb the powers of the words she'd spoken, the powers of earth.

In the evenings, our house doubled as a store, and long into the night, I could hear the men in the front room playing pool and arguing, slamming things around. I knew I shouldn't be afraid. Mammie had a gun, and I knew the place she kept it. I knew how to hold it, how to shoot if things got rough. But beneath my bed were jugs and jugs of the clear liquor the men came to buy, the spirits that made their eyes grow wild and their pulses dull. Sometimes when the supply ran low, Mammie, who was her own best customer, would let a man inside to fetch more, telling him with a phlegmatic laugh where she hid it. The men would bring me presents and kneel beside my bed. Once a man brought me a Bible with a hard wood cover, and he'd whittled my name into the wood. When I turned to thank him, I saw that his eyes were wet and full of pus like a wormy dog's.

"Mammie," I called out, scared. I could hear her cackling above the music in the other room.

"Shhh," the man said. His breath burned my ear. He licked his broken lips. Through the cracks in the ceiling, I could see hints of stars. I stared at them while he ran his hands through my hair. "Mammie," I cried again.

"Hey, Bo," she hollered back, "don't take no more than you pay for."

Some nights the men never left the store. They slept out on the porch with the chickens and began their drinking again as soon as the sun came up.

On those mornings, I took to the woods. Some days I carried a book, but usually I played in the trees, swinging on my vines, pretending to forget. I imagined myself wrapping vines around the necks of the drunk men who came to my bed. Around and around.

On one of those days, Mammie called me to her, said that I had to come out of the woods and comb the tangles from my hair like a girl and be content to work in her store.

"No, no, Mammie," I begged, "I'm too little."

"Y'ain't little no more," she told me, running her hand over my rounding breasts. "Ten year old—er maybe 'leven. Time to put you to work."

"Please, no," I stammered. "They'll bother me."

"Who you mean?"

"The men."

"They ain't gone hurt you," she fussed. "You'll get used to it."

I started crying, and Mammie, who never learned the value of tears, told me to hush. We were in the backyard, right next to the water faucet, and when I couldn't silence myself, Mammie jerked me up by one arm and grabbed the water hose. She whipped me across the back with the hose until a fight broke out in the front yard and she had to go run off the men who, days-drunk, had taken up residence on the doorsteps.

When she dropped my arm, I ran from her to the tool shed and gathered large nails and a mallet so heavy it hurt my arms to tote it. I climbed up my vine and broke the bark off the trees within my reach. "I *hate* them," I cried. "I hate them all." I beat holes in those trees, hammering in the nails and then wiggling them around and around. I knocked holes right through the middle of the vine until I could split it up the middle with my hands. "I hope they *die*," I blurted out to the woods. "I'd rather die than work there."

I wasn't yet finished when I heard Mammie calling. "Jael? Get in this house, Jael."

I ignored her and continued to destroy my quiet spot.

A little later, I heard her calling again, "Jael? Don't make me come after you, gal."

But I stayed in the woods. I was tired from all the hammering, and the anger had almost left me. I wanted to take a bath, to go to sleep, but I knew there'd be no rest for me once I went inside that place. Mammie'd punish me—or get one of those men to do it for her. Darkness was bearing down, and I knew that Mammie was too rickety to give me much trouble when I could dodge her blows between pine trees. I dropped to the ground, the mallet zipped up inside my jacket.

I heard her rustling the leaves on the ground as she walked down the path I'd made to my sacred place. I leaned against the tree, hoping to be invisible, but knowing the tree couldn't protect me anymore. "I won't go back there," I whispered to myself.

Just as she stepped into my view, I heard Mammie muttering, "Hit's your last chance, girl. I'm breakin' the switch right now. Gone tear your hide up."

She stepped right up to the vines where she knew I played. Placing one withered hand on the thickest vine that I had broken at the center, she looked up to the tree limbs where I so often sat.

Quickly, I stepped from behind the tree and knocked her over the head with my mallet.

I hit her too hard.

I ran to the house, slamming the screen door, and headed straight for the front room where the men would be meeting for drinks within the hour. I climbed onto the shelf behind the bar, hiding behind stacks of paper bags. In the dark, I gnawed my fingernails down to the nubs, sucking clean the dirt and bloody remnants of my cuticles.

And when the men arrived and began their games, helping themselves to moonshine and paying no notice to Mammie's absence, I eased myself onto the ground, put on her apron, and offered my services.

So I was a ward of the court, and I slept on a cot in the basement of the Pentecostal church until old River Bill, a recently widowed deacon, offered to take me in. The church lady who came to bring me food and extra clothes delivered the news. As she picked the nits out of my hair, she said it was a miracle from God that a man like River Bill would take a wild girl like me to raise as his own daughter. She said it was a blessing in disguise— that one of Mammie's regular customers had bashed her brains out in those woods, over a bottle of liquor. According to the church lady, Mammie had reaped what she had sown. She said there was new hope for my heathen soul.

It didn't bother me at all for one of those men to take the blame for my crime. It was their fault. And I knew they'd never pay for half the crimes they committed. I blamed them completely.

River Bill picked me up one blustery morning in his green truck and carried me back to Mammie's house where I collected my big winter coat, my wood-covered Bible, and my Mammie's black rubber shoes that she wore in the rain. I looked everywhere for her dark books written in the old alphabet, but they were not on the shelf where she'd kept them. I saw her clay pitchers shattered on the kitchen floor. I picked up my snake-beating stick on the way out. When River Bill saw my stick, he told me to throw it down, that there were plenty of other sticks where we were going, but I didn't. Being of gentle spirit, he let me bring it along.

Although I was afraid of River Bill, I liked him. I'd never had a father before. I'd always wanted one. The woman from the church said he never drank, and when he smiled at me, he didn't mock me with his teeth.

On that first day, we drove deep into the woods, along sandy, single-laned roads, curving between the stubby pin oaks that were made midgets by the grainy, white soil. From time to time, we'd cross makeshift bridges, and I'd hold my breath knowing that if River Bill turned that steering wheel just an inch too far, we'd sink into the murky swamp. You're supposed to *trust* him, I told my-self. The woman from the church said I could trust him. But the words didn't keep my legs from trembling.

We went through great holes that bounced us high enough to bump our heads on the top of the cab. And sometimes, large branches would slap into the open window and sting my arm.

When we reached the landing, River Bill parked his truck up on the sandy hill, and we walked down to the river's amber edge.

"Put on them rubber boots," he told me, and so I did, fitting them over my shoes.

I stood at the edge of the water and examined the transparent minnows swimming around my feet. River Bill pulled his boat out of the bushes, and the green wooden structure floated over to where I stood.

"Hop in," he said, and spitting tobacco, he pulled his cap down hard on his head.

I sat on the box where River Bill kept his catch. He sat at the back of the boat and pushed us off the ground with a paddle. Then he turned the boat around, cranked the motor, and sped off down the river.

I hadn't ridden in a boat with a motor before. It made me cold, and bugs splattered up against my head. I had to peel them off my skin with my fingers. On either side of us stood looming mossy trees whose shadows wavered and shone in the black water.

Soon we came to a place where it seemed the river ended, and River Bill slowed the boat down.

"You all right?" he asked, and I nodded.

"We got to go through a little rough place here. Just hold on."

And he turned the boat into a forest that had grown up in spite of the river. If I'd stuck my arms out, I could have touched the trees on either side of us.

"Duck your head," he'd say before we puttered beneath low-lying limbs. And occasionally, he'd jerk the boat to the left or right to avoid a cypress knee in the middle of our path.

Then we hit open water again, and River Bill gave the motor some gas, and I couldn't hear anything but the motor's hum and the wind against my face.

River Bill lived in a house built over the water. He ran a little store for fishermen, and I worked there for the next ten years, only leaving the river for trips to the grocery store or to church.

We bought the same groceries every two weeks: corn meal and flour, rice and sugar, eggs and bacon and milk. River Bill didn't speak to me in public, but placed the boxes and wrappers in my arms one by one as he pulled them from the grocery shelves.

When we went to church on Sunday mornings, we wore old clothes in the boat, carrying our Sunday things in a plastic bag to keep them dry. We got dressed on the hill behind the open doors of the truck and left our damp clothes hanging from tree limbs like waving ghosts.

In the truck, I recited Bible verses to River Bill to please him. Though Mammie had not been a God-fearing woman, I'd studied some scripture at school, and she'd let me keep the testament given to me as a gift years before. It occurred to me that a deacon's daughter should know the word of God. So I learned it.

At church, I sat with River Bill and envied the children my own age who all sat together towards the back.

I remembered some of them from school. They still
frowned at me. Every Sunday when River Bill rose to
pass the collection plate, I thought about switching
seats. But those children stared with questioning, serious eyes when I passed. They'd never been able to figure
me out. They didn't even want to try anymore.

Once after the service, when people were shaking
hands, a Sunday school teacher invited me to join her
teenager class that met on Sunday evenings. River Bill
explained that we lived too far away.

We also lived too far away from the nearest school.
Since there was no way for the bus to get to me, I wasn't
required to go. The school district packed boxes with
books and study sheets, and we picked up my lessons
from town whenever we went. Once a month, I met with
a teacher, Mr. Stanwick, who gave me tests and pro-
moted me to the next chapter or level or grade. Learning
came easy for me. I completed two or three grades every
year until Mr. Stanwick didn't have anything else for me
to study.

After that, I studied the books I found in boxes in the
back of a closet. There were Sunday school quarterlies
stacked in piles and bound with twine, and there were
books of literature with hard covers and tiny words filling the hundreds of pages. Inside every cover, River
Bill's wife had written her name in black ink, her signature angular and tall. Some days I sat for hours memo-
rizing the slant of her letters. I almost felt I knew her
through those books—the tiny square ones on manners
and embroidery mixed with the picture books of flowers,
the magazines about primitive men, bones jutting from
their noses. She read so many different things but always

signed her name the same way. I thought she would have made a good mother for me.

River Bill's house was on stilts, and it had a large wooden porch with a floating dock attached. On the porch, he kept an ice chest full of drinks. In a refrigerator, he kept paper cups of bait and packs of crackers in plastic wrappers. And he had a small stock of fishing lures and weights and hooks and lines and flies in bright colors. He sold boat gas. River Bill put me in charge of the store. Sometimes customers came every few hours, and sometimes nobody came for days. Still, I sat on the dock, my cane pole in one hand and a book in the other, listening to the mudfish jump, to the awful, soul-sick cries of bullfrogs. I didn't mind sitting outside—even in winter.

Since River Bill fished all day and dug his bait in the early evening, I had great spans of time to myself. Sometimes I'd paddle out in the one-man boat into the narrow paths between trees and logs. Sometimes I'd carry my radio that River Bill brought me from town, and I'd play it for the alligators very loudly, and I'd say, "Do you hear that, you big scaly clod?" But I didn't get too close.

I liked to paddle underneath the house. When the river was low, I could scratch pictures into the green algae-slipperiness on the stilts.

In the evenings when River Bill came home, I'd hold his boat steady while he'd climb out, and I'd secure the craft to a hook in the dock as he told me how many he'd caught. I'd carry the fish over to a table and scrape their scales off with a spoon, split their bellies with my pocketknife, and rip the guts away with my fingers. Then River

Bill would fry them in a cast-iron skillet along with corn dodgers. We'd eat on the dock, sitting in our rocking chairs and watching the sky. River Bill liked to eat the tails, so I'd give him mine in exchange for his fish roe, so orange and salty and good.

Before bed, I'd cut him a slice of the pound cake that I baked every Saturday, and River Bill would read aloud from the Bible. I didn't tell him when he mispronounced words. Sometimes I didn't know how to say them either, but I knew when he said them wrong.

Some days I didn't listen as he read. Instead, I tried to remember the names of plants Mammie had taught me. I couldn't always recall her language, but I knew the shapes of the leaves.

We slept in the same room. There were two beds pushed up against opposite walls, with a night table beside each bed. On the table beside his bed, River Bill kept a picture of his wife when she was young. I left the table beside my bed just the way it was when I arrived— with the picture of Jesus on the cross.

During my first winter with River Bill, I began wearing his dead wife's bathrobe in the early mornings when I rose to start the coffee. Then as I outgrew my clothes, I rifled through a chest and found some of her things that almost fit. So I wore them, smelling of cedar and age.

I'm not exactly sure when I became his wife instead of his daughter, but it confused me like nothing before. It did not make me mad; it made me hot and restless and lonely. I tolerated it so long as he had cleaned his mouth of tobacco. He was a toughened man who could have beaten me but never did, and I knew it couldn't be a sin since he prayed at night and woke singing hymns in praise of each red sunrise.

River Bill had a year-round brownness about the skin on his arms and face and neck, but beneath the white T-shirts, he grew paler and soft. Since he always wore work boots that laced over his ankles, his feet were the strangest of all. They were oyster-white, and the tough, callused heels looked as though they could be flaked away. What I hated most was the smell of those feet. River Bill wore shoes even when he waded. So his feet carried the sweet rotting odor of something soaked, then dried, then soaked again. His feet were always sour.

Nights when he climbed into my bed, heaving his weight onto me, it was the scent of those hairy, white feet that sickened me most. I could forget about the wheezing, about the clicking in the back of his throat, about the madness swirling around inside me each time he pushed his way in, but the smell stayed with me, even when I pretended to be a leaf. Even when I sent myself floating out the window and over the black river.

There was more to the smell than his feet.

Later when he was gone, I'd think of the way his toes had brushed my legs. I'd look over to him snoring in the next bed and choke on the memory of his toe-touch.

Our house was an island, the only dry place in the entire wet world. I pretended sometimes that there was no one else on the planet. I played Noah, pretending I was on a mission from God.

I stayed dry for days at a time, and then sometimes, impulsively, I'd open the bedroom window, perch on the ledge, and dive. I never knew for sure if the water would be deep enough or if I'd hit bottom, maybe split my head on a root. It was risky, but it was the only thing that called my insides to attention. When I was on that ledge, getting ready to drop, I woke up. Leaping from that window made the world vivid. It was the one thing that assured me I was real.

In the water, I'd swim so far, so hard, that my muscles cramped up. I treasured the cramps, the aliveness of pain, the immediacy. Sometimes I'd let myself shout, and sometimes I distracted myself by thinking about wetness and dryness and what it all meant. It only took a moment to get wet—splash, an instant soaking. But drying out was different altogether. I'd pull myself onto the dock, peel off the wet clothes, and stand naked in the wind, feeling dampness sticking to me, holding its grudge. Like everything else in the world, wetness resists change. I avoided towels and let the drying come slowly. I didn't want to miss it. I wanted to remember how it felt.

We had big storms on the river. Late afternoons we'd watch clouds collecting in the east, turning from gray to wicked and moving in. I liked storms more than anything, envied their power, their showy ways. River Bill claimed that his house was as sturdy as any house built on land, so we sat them out even though people from church said we were crazy. We'd open up the windows so the wind wouldn't blow out the panes, and River Bill would send me into the hall where I was out of danger. But he stood in the front room, the wind whipping through, and he watched as the trees did backbends. Sometimes the rain blew inside and left puffy streaks on the paneling.

One year the rains fell every day for a week, and the river rose higher and higher. I watched as the water creeped up the stilts. The house was a little girl holding up her Sunday dress. The river was about to wet her underpants. That's how it felt—like something private, thrilling, and dangerous. I checked every hour to see how close we were to washing away.

River Bill laughed at me and told me about a time when he was a boy living in that place with his parents. He said a storm came and lifted the house off the stilts and washed it down the river. But this house was sturdy, he said. This house wouldn't sail. He'd built it himself. And it couldn't rain forever.

I could see worry on his face. In the night, he stood near the window, looking out at the rain, and he called "God Almighty" under his breath.

The morning that I sat in the window and dangled my feet in the water, River Bill bowed down to the storm. Ill-tempered, he told me to get inside, and then he ordered me to pack a bag with extra clothes, another one with food. He boarded up the windows in spite of the winds, and I packed towels in the windowsills. Then we ran out across the slippery dock and jumped in the boat. The rain blurred everything but colors. We watched the sky bruise darker.

River Bill cranked the motor, and we drove wide-open away. The water bubbled beneath us, and the heaviness in the air almost sank the boat. River Bill dodged the falling trees as the storm chased us to the land. If I could have opened my mouth, I would have screamed. My face felt like something stretched tight for framing.

When we got to the landing, water had almost taken over the high ground where River Bill's truck was parked. He drove the boat right up onto the sand and shouted, "Run for it," but the turbulence muffled his words.

"What?" I shouted back, and he shoved me out of the boat as hard as he could.

The wind knocked me down, but eventually I managed to crawl under the pickup. River Bill wiggled on his belly beside me, put his arm around me, and pushed my head down. Even under the truck we could hear trees cracking like thousands of knuckles. I concentrated on the earth, the individual blue grains of sand in the middle of all those white ones. The tornado touched down in a circle around us, and River Bill whispered, "Sweet Jesus." I knew that a tornado could lift the blue sand right out of the white grains if it wanted. But I wasn't afraid. Not for a minute.

We stayed with the preacher's family for a week. River Bill had to buy a new boat, but when the river suaged down, he and the preacher went to see if the house was still standing.

It was.

So we moved back home. The place was a mess. When we stepped on the rugs, water gushed up around our feet. I took the broom, and River Bill took the measuring tape. While I swept the wetness out, he wrote down sizes for new boards, new carpet. Then he took the boards off the windows, and I wrung out the drapes, and he said he was proud of me for being able to handle a crisis. We sang "Old Susannah" and "Little Brown Jug," and River Bill even pulled down his zither and played for a few minutes, but then he went back to work. In spite of all the damage, he felt good. I could tell because he talked and talked and ran his hand through my hair as he passed me.

In the afternoon, he told me fishing stories and asked if I'd ever set a hopper hook.

"What?" I asked.

"A hopper hook," he repeated. "When the water's high, you bait a hook and hang it from a tree, and big bass jump up for the bait. I never taught you how to fish with a hopper hook?"

"No."

"Well, since it's a special occasion, I say we go fishing."

So we put away the tools, climbed in the new boat, and floated out to a nearby oak. We were closer to the limbs than usual and could reach them without even having to stand up. River Bill tied the line to the tree limb, baited the hook, and told me to paddle gently. I moved us away.

"Got to be real still," he said.

"Is this legal?" I asked.

"No, no," he answered. "I haven't done this in years." And he grinned. "Only on special occasions."

We waited there silently. I started daydreaming, and I guess River Bill noticed. He whispered, "Watch it, now."

After a few minutes, a big trout exploded out of the water and caught the hook in its mouth.

"Did you see that?" River Bill shouted. "We got her." He paddled us over to the fish pendulum and yanked her mouth from the hook. "One more time."

When we'd caught two big bass, we cut the line and went back to the house. I cleaned and cooked the fish while River Bill climbed onto the roof to replace some shingles.

He works hard, I told myself. He doesn't drink. He goes to church. He lives in harmony with the river. He only takes his share.

I liked him more that day than any other. In bed that night, I hated myself for imagining the ways he might die.

At River Bill's store, we had regular customers who knew me and stopped by sometimes just to say hello. Some of them teased me, commenting on the size of my breasts. If I didn't keep my hair pulled up, one of the men would tug it playfully, and there was always someone pinching me and winking when I turned around.

But I looked forward to their visits in spite of their

teasing because they always brought me gifts from town. Everyone on the river knew I loved to read, so they'd come with old magazines that their wives had clipped recipes from. They brought me books and newspapers. One man even gave me volumes of an encyclopedia, one at a time, and all I had to do in return was flirt with him, let him run his hand across my backside and then jerk away, acting surprised.

It was easy work that wore me down.

But River Bill rarely brought me anything. He made his way into my space as often as he liked. He was gentle and never hurt me, but I hated it just the same. Each time, I gritted my teeth, swam orange in the pool behind my eyes. Each time, I felt my lungs flutter and contract. I swallowed the tears like medicine. And howls.

There was never a gift for me the next day. Not even a feather or a piece of bark. I would have taken anything at all.

One warm May morning, I was fishing off the dock and reading a week-old newspaper when I heard an approaching motor cut down to a putter, and the smell of gasoline whiffed me out of my reverie. I stood and waved to a fisherman I'd never seen before. He tossed me his rope, and when I bent down to knot it through the hook, he said, "Nice tits."

For a minute, I stared at his big grinning face, and then, on an impulse, thinking only that he hadn't brought me a gift, I unhooked the rope and threw it back, pushing the front end of his high-class boat away.

The man was already standing, and my shove caused him to lose his balance. He stumbled backwards, catching himself with his hands as he passed the seat.

"Hey," he yelled. "Hey, wait. I'm sorry." And he paddled back up to the dock. He was short and muscular, wearing only cutoff blue jeans. I let him secure the boat himself.

I walked up to the porch because my face felt flushed, but I had this strange urge to laugh. I didn't want him to see my expression.

"I know I deserved that," he said. "I'm real sorry. I hope you'll forget it."

"What can I get for you?" I asked him, turning around so quickly it surprised him into a smile.

"I need some jelly worms if you got any."

"How many?"

"About two packs."

Even after I walked away to get his jelly worms, the man kept talking.

"I could use a Coca-Cola, too, while you're in there."

"Go ahead and get it," I yelled back. "They're in that first cooler—the blue one."

By the time I got back, the man was sitting in my rocking chair, opening his Coke with the end of his pocketknife.

"Name's Thompie Hayes," he said, and he stuck a cigarette in the corner of his mouth.

"You owe me three dollars, Thompie."

"Yes, ma'am," he muttered, his eyes glimmering like guilt. He pulled a handful of crumpled dollars out of his pocket, straightened out three of them, and put them in my hand. He didn't let go of the money right away.

As I slipped the dollars in my pocket, I looked down at his brown feet and envied the way his veins wrapped around his muscles like packaging tape.

"Oh, I forgot to charge you for the Coke," I said.

"You'll have to charge me for two. I got one out for you."

I looked at him hard and instinctively pulled my hand up to the stretched neckline of my T-shirt.

"You got a name?" he asked me.

"Jael."

"That's a place for criminals. What's your name?"

"J-A-E-L," I said, spelling it for him. "That's my name."

"Well, Jael, if you're not too busy, why don't you sit down and talk awhile."

"I *am* busy," I claimed.

"Doing what?" he replied, and I shrugged.

"Don't make yourself so comfortable," I told him. I liked the way his chest muscles moved when he lifted his drink or just shifted his arms. I hoisted myself onto the porch railing.

Thompie was young—maybe twenty-five—with short dark hair that got curly around the edges. He had wide blue eyes and dark skin and a small fishhook scar on one cheek. When he smiled, I noticed that one of his front teeth overlapped the other one.

"Did you know you've got polka-dotted knees?" he asked.

"Freckles," I laughed. "So what?"

"Oh, nothing."

He paused, and I looked at him in the eyes until he looked away.

"So what's it like, living out here on the river?"

Behind me I could hear the crickets calling from their wire container home, already doomed to death by hook.

"I like it," I said too slowly.

"Is that all you can say?" he teased. "That you like it?"

"I like it," I said again, smiling back.

I imagined what River Bill would think if he saw me propped up like a queen, my head tilted back, laughing with a stranger. For a moment, I wanted him to catch me that way. He'd never even seen me. He didn't even know who I was.

"So you live here with your family?"

"Sort of."

"You got brothers or sisters?"

I shook my head. In the distance, I could hear another motor, and I was glad when it died away.

"Wait, wait, wait one minute," Thompie said, shifting to the edge of the rocker. "You ain't married, are you?"

Instantly I felt something inside that I'd never felt before. It began in my chest, tingled through my stomach like a chill, and shook its way out between my legs. At first, I thought it must be lust, but it felt more like loss.

Again, I shook my head, and when Thompie sat back and resumed rocking, I started flirting back.

"So where's your wife today?" I asked, and I looked down at my fingernails, nibbled to the quick.

"I'm not married."

"Then your girlfriend. Where's she?"

"Don't have a girlfriend, either," he answered, but I saw his blush, and I noticed his dimples caving into his mouth.

"Oh, yes, you do. I've seen you out here on this river with her before," I lied, hopping down from my perch.

"I never been this far down the river in my life," he answered. "You must have seen somebody that looked like me."

"Well, what are you doing out here now?"

Thompie grabbed me by the shoulders, smirked, and guided me into the chair.

"You changed the subject," he retorted, one dimple caving in. "We were talking about you. And I already got you figured out, Miss Jael. Your mamma's dead, ain't she? And you live alone here with your daddy. You sit up here on this porch and tend the store and read books. Books about everything. Sometimes your relatives float in for a fish fry, but mostly it's just you and nature. That right?"

"Who told you that?"

"I guess you could say I pieced it together. Truth is, I come from a town about a hundred miles up the river. I been camping and fishing my way down. The people on the water know about your daddy's store, and they sure know about you. You're a regular legend, Miss Jael. Is all that stuff true?"

"The truth doesn't really have much to do with anything now, does it?" I teased, cocking my head.

"I can drive a boat better than you ever hoped to," I told him, and I gave the Evinrude motor so much gas at once that we bounced up off the dark water and skipped down the river like a tiny flat stone.

Thompie's boat was a bass boat, a sleek brown-and-green blend with fiberglass sides and cushioned vinyl seats. Truthfully, I'd never driven anything so strong or so large, and I certainly had never driven a boat with a steering wheel and a seat for the driver at the front rather than in the rear. But I didn't feel compelled to be particularly truthful to Thompie. His boat even had a windshield, and it occurred to me that I shouldn't trust a sportsman who was afraid to get bits of dragonflies on his body.

All afternoon we parted the open waters, driving in one direction, full speed ahead. We didn't even stop to fish. We passed beneath bridges, and we zipped by sand bars. When the sun dropped low in the sky, we docked at a sandy deserted landing. Thompie said we'd probably crossed state lines, and I felt triumphant for no particular reason.

I pulled the boat up into the murky edge of the water, into the bushes. It wasn't until Thompie warned me not to scratch the bottom that I felt a tinge of homesickness for River Bill.

We found a tiny camper parked on the beach amid the trees. In one window, someone had carved out a sign that said LIAR'S JUNCTION. While Thompie unloaded the cooler of drinks and fish that we borrowed from River Bill, I checked the camper door. It was unlocked.

Except for the water moccasin coiled up in the kitchen sink, the place was uninhabited. We borrowed cookware from the camper and sat outside beneath the trees while our fish slowly bubbled in the borrowed grease. In the white river sand, Thompie dug me a little bed, and undressed me and put me in it. He covered me with his own body, and no bugs bit me all night long.

When I first woke up, daylight glared in my face, so I rolled over to protect myself from the sun's intrusive rays. I slept again. The next time I woke, I could feel dry sand in my eyes. I sat up, spit on my fingers, and rubbed the thin lids until the burning became unbearable.

"Thompie," I called, squinting. "Can you come here?"

I waited for an answer, but hearing nothing, I rose, vision blurry, and wandered to the river and waded out. The water was still cold, and I could feel my skin toughen in response, my breathing hesitant. Finally I dove under, cleaning my eyes beneath the surface. When I came up for air, I rubbed loose dirt from my limbs while my eyes slowly focused. And I rinsed my mouth with water, so good and flavored with old.

Then I looked to the place where the boat had been tied and saw that it was missing.

"Thompie," I yelled, "Thompie, I'm awake now."

I listened for the motor to crank, assuming he was fishing nearby, but heard nothing. So I trudged towards the hill and sat at the place where water gently lapped at the sand.

I didn't have anything to do until Thompie returned except watch the minnows flit about like living slivers of sticks. I looked to see if he'd left a pole for me to fish with. Since he hadn't, I waited. Gradually it occurred to me that he would have left the cooler behind if he'd only gone out to catch our lunch. I investigated the landing and found my clothes left in a small heap. Even the pans we'd taken from the camper were missing. For a moment, I felt my lungs lift, desperately, like wings, and a soft noise escaped my throat before I settled back down. There was a stinging in my stomach that I'd never felt before.

I thought maybe I was hungry.

I searched the woods for a long time looking for the right stick—a stick comparable to the one I'd left behind at River Bill's. I couldn't remember why I'd left River Bill's—it wasn't like me at all. I hadn't been angry with him. He hadn't done anything wrong. But I needed a stick. I had to keep my head clear. I needed a stick straight enough to function as a staff and sturdy enough to sustain the impact of hard blows. Most important, it had to be long enough for me to hold it in my hands and beat the brains out of any snakes I encountered without putting me in their striking range.

Snakes—and alligators, wildcats, parasites, poison oak. What I needed was a magic wand, not a stick, and panic slapped me with every branch as I wandered among the trees. You could die out here, I thought, and I whimpered like an animal. I yelled, "Thompie Hayes, you're an asshole." It didn't help.

I sat down on the soggy ground and tried to remember what Thompie looked like. I wasn't sure, and I cried for a minute and felt it in my lungs, the danger of crying that way. I knew I had to stop. So I breathed deep and watched an orange bug meander up the bark of a water oak. Little tiny bug. Doesn't feel a thing. I consoled myself, following its path with my eyes.

But then the snakes were back, in my mind, everywhere, and I couldn't slow my breathing down. Stop it, I whispered. Stop it now.

I'd read in a magazine about people in the rain forests of Asia who played with cobras. When they saw a coiled cobra, they stood back and took a stick and drew circles on the ground around the snake. And the snake uncoiled, following the movement of the stick. When the snake was entirely uncoiled and had lost its spring, the person smacked the snake on top of the head, driving its fangs into the ground and milking out the venom. And then the snake had no power for a while. Even children could play with cobras if they knew how to milk them.

I could do that, I thought. I could milk a rattlesnake if I needed to. Or a water moccasin. If I had a stick.

So I found one.

The stick I discovered was actually a tree, and I mourned sacrificing it as I twisted the narrow trunk and then pounded it in half with a rock. But the sun had already peaked, and I knew it might take time to prepare my hunting equipment.

Again I sat at the edge of the river, this time sharpening one end of my stick with the dull rock. No boats

passed all afternoon. Whenever fear slipped up on me,
I hummed under my breath, "Dull, dull, dull, dull." It
made a sound like a river creature, like a new breed of
frog or cricket. I hummed it until I became only slightly
concerned about whether or not I would eat before
sleeping or where I would sleep at all. By late afternoon,
the tip of my stick was arrow-sharp and ready to split the
rubbery backs of bullfrogs. So I made my way into the
swampy place where earth and water overlap.

I had to move slowly between bushes and reeds,
stepping gently in hopes of avoiding broken bottles that
had settled beneath the soft ground. The mossy oaks
cast thick shadows, and I held my stick above my shoulder, prepared to swing down on any alligator I met
accidently in the bog.

The croaking frogs mocked me as I tossed my spear
into the reeds and pulled it out empty again and again.
Mosquitoes buzzed about my neck, and I slapped them
away, splatting my body with foul-smelling mud. At last,
I stabbed into the murkiness and felt it resist, then pierce
that frog-toughness I'd been waiting for. I managed to
spear two more before the afternoon hazed away.

Though I knew that snakes had claimed the camper,
I also knew that I needed matches to light a cooking fire.
So I ventured inside the trailer and quickly rummaged
through cabinets and drawers, retrieving matches and
also some fishing line to use later. And I promised myself that I'd never open that heavy camper door again.

Frogs are easy to clean because only their legs are
edible. But cleaning them without a knife is difficult
indeed. Between my lack of utensils and a fire that re-

sisted its own wood, I didn't eat until it was past dark. I didn't care. I hummed my song, ate them half-raw, and didn't taste anything anyway.

The days that followed were busy ones as I fished and familiarized myself with the surrounding land, but they were easy days, too. By the second morning, the fear was gone. The anger was gone. Thompie's face was such a blur that I couldn't have picked him out of a police lineup if I'd needed to. Nothing was left but the song, "Dull, dull, dull, dull." Sometimes I sang it fast and loud like a bird, and sometimes I stretched each syllable like a bee, and sometimes I listened to the quiet cadence of it and wondered where it came from. For a while, I waited in the spot where Thompie had deserted me, but that place became too oppressive, and with someone else's camper parked there, I knew I could never make myself at home. So I vowed to find more suitable ground.

On a woods exploration, I came to a place where a tornado had ripped through, overturning some trees and transplanting others. One great oak had resisted the storm, had, in fact, merely leaned into it so that half of its roots were pulled from the earth and the other half remained planted. The result was a large hole in the ground with an awning of tree trunk and roots. The underside of the upturned tree reminded me of a wrinkled old hag, and the thin and broken roots hanging from dirt masses looked like nymph hair. My instinct was to drop to my knees and sculpt a face for her. I had to crawl into the crater to begin my work. As I molded, the dirt sprinkled down on my head in a fine earthy rain.

After a while I abandoned the hag's face and began dragging the soil out of the hole with my hands until I had both created and decorated my new home. That night I slept beneath the giant oak, curled up against a wall of wood. The vinelike roots that blocked the moon from my view formed my doorway.

To me that tree, that home, smelled just the same as the river, only dryer, and it seemed that I could feel the earth's moisture flow through my body and pass into the tree's vascular system. And I was just another limb. Nothing more.

My intercourse with the outside world had been limited my whole life, so I didn't particularly miss having human contacts. I had always considered the river superior comp. ny, and it wasn't until sometime later that I began to think about other people. The first time, I was asleep under the mothering tree when I felt water creeping beneath my belly and woke to an early morning storm. As the lightning cracked outside, I recalled the eyes of those men in Mammie's store, all watery and hungry, their work-tough fingers aching to graze my breasts as they passed me. Or the ones who came to my bed and told me how the cold had taken their whole arms, how they needed to warm them beneath my covers. How I let them.

I remembered the faces of those church children, calm and tamed. The way they looked at me, their clean heads tilted, told me they knew I wasn't a child, my body only an illusion. And though we studied the same scripture, recited together "Knock and the door shall be opened unto you," they knew their doors led to different places than mine.

That same day I took the sharp end of my stick and engraved a cross with two bloody little cross-beams into the inside of my thigh. I hummed to myself as I carved, and my song numbed the pain until I hardly felt it at all, and I was glad there was a place for the blackness in me to drain out if it was ready for draining.

I went about my work as usual, fishing in the river and sharpening my tools on stones, collecting sticks to hammer into the earth around my tree-cave, to build a fortress of sorts—a sign to alert the foxes that my dugout was inhabited already. And though I tried to keep busy, I couldn't free my mind of disturbing thoughts. I kept picturing River Bill, serene and good-hearted but no stranger to my groin, and I imagined myself placing his graying head into my lap and then bashing at his temples with sharp rocks, back and forth, one hand at a time, until his own evils poured out in a bloody soup.

Eventually, I decided to soak myself in the river and cool the swirling anger that felt like it spun up and gathered around my head in a white halo rage. So I ran down the hill and towards the water, hardly stopping when I tripped over a stump and gashed my knee. My feet flew over the grassy bank, and I dove desperately, and I splashed into that muddy hole, yelling and yelling as the water burned into my fresh cuts.

In a dream I saw Mammie on the ground where I'd left her, and she was a ghost, but she couldn't get up. She was flinging her arms through the leaves and pine straw, and her dead face was covered with red bugbites, and there was a buzzard nesting in her hair, pecking at her neck.

"Mammie," I called, "I didn't mean to leave you there."

But she couldn't hear me.

"Mammie," I said, "I'm sorry."

I reached up and felt the tree roots dangling over my face, and rolled over. It was still dark outside.

They buried her, I told myself. She didn't stay in the woods for long. Some old drunk went out to pee and found her that same night.

But when I closed my eyes again, she was back. It was like Mammie was inside of me. And I was the one who was buried.

I marked myself in other ways, dipping the prickly ends of sand-spurs into berry juice and then jabbing those spurs into the soft skin on the inside of my arm. I drew a purple crescent moon and also a tiny star.

As my cuts tried to heal, I picked the scabs away and ate them, day after day, relishing the salty, crispy hardness. Each evening after cooking, I'd straddle the trunk of my leaning tree and carve a fresh notch in my body.

I came to love thick skin—the durability of my own heels and my leathery, dry lips. I aimed to cultivate scars in pretty patterns of my own design. I etched my name onto one hip bone to remind myself that I had a name. The curvy letter was hardest.

The days ran together as they became hotter. Sometimes the sun baked into my head so hot that it put me to sleep wherever I happened to be sitting. And when afternoon storms whipped gusts of hot air through the woods and then drove that air into the ground with mighty pounding rain, I whooped and danced and praised the stinging drops that drenched me.

Hungry for more than fish each day, I devised my own trapping system, digging deep holes into the earth and covering them with thin layers of weeds and leaves. After a couple of days, I began to catch an occasional squirrel or rabbit. Captured animals can be vicious, and killing them down in the hole turned out to be more difficult than catching them. Usually, I knocked them in the head with a large stone. Once I was bitten.

I developed an interest in bones and began collecting the bleached-out remnants of animals that I found beneath shrubs. When chiseled correctly, the leg bones of small animals made particularly good spoons. With practice, I became quite an artisan. In my spare time, I even designed jewelry for myself, roping vertebrae on to the thinnest grapevines and tying them around my wrists and neck and waist.

It was probably midsummer when, after spending a morning on the riverbank and catching nothing, I trudged up the hill towards my tree-cave, hungry and destined to dine on huckleberries and mushrooms.

There were always leaves, of course, to suck the life from when the water's quick rising kept fish from biting. Mammie had taught me to protect myself against poisonous plants. You put a leaf on your tongue, she'd said, and leave it there for half an hour. If it doesn't make your mouth burn, it's safe to eat. I could always eat clover flowers, but they never made me full.

When I reached my plot, I thought I heard voices but assumed my imagination was taking advantage of the heat and my hunger. Then I heard high-pitched laughter pealing through the woods. It occurred to me that the owners of the camper might be nearby. I figured they were hunters and possibly dangerous, so I withdrew into my cool dirt room.

One part of me wanted to stay safe inside, but another part wanted to scout out the place and see the people who'd come so near. Though I knew that hunters might mistake me for an animal and shoot me by accident, and though I figured that at the very least, they'd take me back to River Bill, I still wanted to see a person, to talk to another person, to tell them my name and hear them say it aloud.

I wondered if my words would make sense to them. I opened my mouth to test my tongue, but all it would say was "dull, dull."

I gnawed down my toenails and ran my fingers through my long, knotted hair. Then I slipped outside and into the thicket, making my way towards the landing where I'd first arrived.

From the trees, I watched them. There were three women, none of them particularly young, but not old either. They had erected a large tent and gathered wood for a fire that wasn't yet lit. Their backpacks were dropped on the ground, but I didn't see a vehicle. One woman had long, straight, black hair and olive skin and a thin body. She knelt in the dirt, whittling. The second woman was short and bony with flamy red hair that wisped up around her face. She ambled at the edge of the river, barefoot and playing a wooden flute. The third woman sat with her back to a tree and filled a small pipe and smoked it. She turned her face up to the clouds, eyes closed, and blew out, then placed the pipe on the ground, lifted the thick tip of her single braid and rubbed it over her lips.

I dropped to the ground and stretched out on my belly to observe them in their quiet. They couldn't see me because I stayed behind the leaves of trees and bushes and vines, but if it'd been winter, I'd have been caught most certainly. And I remembered those times in the woods at Mammie's when I'd stripped branches just to keep the leaves from blocking my space. I had to question my judgment then, before I'd known the importance of hiding.

The whittler stood and stripped off her jeans, then her tank top, and I was amazed at her body, its smoothness and the gentle curve of her breasts and the deep-plum darkness of her nipples. I had never seen a woman's body before. She walked out into the water, splashing, and then laughing until the smoker lazily unlaced her boots, rose and stripped. Her body was round with curves, and her hips and thighs reminded me of

horse flanks I'd seen, so muscular and full. As she wandered to the river, slow, she lifted her arms and spun
around, stretched and spread her legs and peed. Then
excited, she called out, "A lily. I pissed a lily."

The other woman continued to blow into her instrument as her friends played, swimming around each
other and dancing in the open water. The notes from her
flute floated high in the air, so hollow and sad, and I felt
an aching that I'd forgotten. I gnawed the bones in my
finger.

Eventually the woman with the straight dark hair
trekked out of the water and sat down in the sand and
rolled until her body was covered. Laughing, she called,
"Amy, put down your flute and swim."

And then the red-haired woman undressed, her
body so boylike but softer. Giggling, she charged towards the water, kicking up earth as her feet grazed the
ground, and the sand-coated one jumped up to race her,
and they splashed for a moment before beginning a song
about listening to the voices of old women. It made me
miss Mammie, a little. It made me feel sorry that I had
hurt her, and it made my head ache. The women
wrapped their arms around each other's necks and
walked in a circle, the water coming up only to their
hips, their hums like lullabies.

When I returned home, it was afternoon, and I felt
sick. I had spent my hunting hours eavesdropping, and
had nothing to eat. For the first time in ages, I cried, but
only one eye had tears. Frustrated, I dragged the
pointed edges of rocks across the skin on my belly, and
I dug my fingernails into my thighs and wept as the
narrow strips of blood dotted up on my leg.

I crawled into my dusty bed, but I couldn't sleep. My mind kept replaying an image, not a dream, and I thought I was running from someone who kept spitting blood on me and the only way to protect myself was to pull at my tongue and stretch it until I could wrap it around my body like a thick coat.

When I woke up, it was still night, and I felt the rumbling of thunder vibrate in my teeth. I backed up deep into my pit, and the tree roots scratched against my back as the rain came hard and the wind whirred through the leaf-loaded limbs of brush.

The wind sounded angry.

But the underground was angry too, hot and waiting for the water's cool to sink low. I tossed beneath my giant oak, sore at the belly from a cut gone crusty and coated in cheesy white.

Years before, Mammie had taught me the healing powers of spit and how to first suck out the poisons and then lick scrapes, flicking my tongue up quickly to clean the wound. But I couldn't lick my own stomach, and the spit I rubbed into the gashed place with my fingers did not seem to hold the same magic.

The storm didn't blow itself out for a long time. Around me I could see the glow as lightning broke into a nearby tree, ravaging it in a second and leaving it to burn at the center.

I remembered seeing pictures in a magazine of people who'd been struck by lightning. Their limbs had turned bluish-brown and were mottled as trees.

It was too dark to look at my own body. I thought my skin looked like a tree already, but I couldn't be sure. I couldn't remember if I'd been struck by lightning. It seemed like a possibility.

Then I heard laughter and loud whoops in the distance, and I remembered the women and imagined their tent, collapsed. Someone yelled out, "Thank you," and I understood her celebration and wanted to join it, but had no energy. I reminded myself that I was different from them. I sang aloud, "Dull, dull, dull, dull," and knew that if I was closer to them, they still wouldn't look my way. I was another life-form. Not like them at all.

I could be their animal, though. I wanted to be their pet. The song wasn't working. I sang it louder.

At dawn, I crawled out into the still-falling rain and made my way down to the river, doubled over. I floated facedown in the dark water and thought, for a moment, about what it would feel like to drown, dropping deeper and deeper into the river, needing to breathe, holding it, widening my eyes in panic and then closing them as though that could somehow protect me from what was imminent. When I stood upright again, I realized I'd done all those things before. I hadn't needed water to create the sensation.

I dug my bait carefully, choosing thick, fat crawlers in hopes of tempting the fish. The rain caused the fish to bite, as rain sometimes will, and within an hour, I'd caught four brim.

Accustomed to summer storms, I'd stashed my wood in the most overgrown part of the thicket, and I retrieved it for my fire. Though slightly damp, the wood burned, and by the time it was hot enough for cooking,

I'd already cleaned my fish. I knew that the camping women might catch scent of my breakfast, but I took my chances. I hadn't yet decided whether or not I wanted to be discovered. And between the infection and my hunger, I didn't have the strength to avoid such a risk.

The wind was in my favor.

After eating, I wandered down to the clearing where the women were camping, and I hid once more behind the greenery. This time, one was picking berries, one was reading, and one drew. I stretched out as quietly as I could, but branches creaked beneath my weight. The redheaded woman looked up from her sketchpad to the place where I rested. But seeing nothing, she continued her work.

I wondered if they had families, if they had left their lovers and children behind to come into the woods for a few days or forever. I wanted them to stay forever or for years, at least. I wondered if they had come from far away or if, in fact, I was very near town and didn't know it. I liked being close to other people—even if they didn't know I was around.

I wondered what it would feel like to be one of their daughters.

An agitated bird began to call out threats, but since birds often squawk, I didn't pay much attention until I heard one of the women cry, "Ouch." I looked towards the berry-picker to see a very angry bluebird swoop down on her head and drag his talons through her black hair. He circled her head and swooped down on her again. By this time, the woman had crouched lower to the ground, as if that could help, and she wrapped her arms about her head like a turban.

The other women jumped up, but they didn't know how to assist. The heavy-hipped woman yelled, "Don't just stand there. Get in the water."

It was a funny sight. One that should be painted, I thought.

The redheaded woman began laughing.

With its feathers all rifled, that bird followed the thin woman all the way to the water's edge. She dove into the river, still dressed, and kept her head under for what seemed to be a full minute. When she resurfaced, the bird had flown back to the trees near the huckleberry bushes. She waded out of the water dripping, her clothes clinging to her narrowness. "I didn't do anything to it," she claimed.

The other women met her as she made her way to the sand.

"Did it hurt you?" the redhead asked, and when the woman shook her head, they all broke into laughter again.

One woman wrung the water out of her T-shirt while the other one inspected the attacked woman's scalp.

Then they all looked over at the bucket of berries, stranded at the battle site.

"I'm not going to get it," the attacked one said.

So the little one draped the wet shirt over her hair for protection and sprinted to the berry bushes, collected the pail, and hurried back towards the camp. The bird didn't bother her at all.

Then all three women sat down beneath the tree,

chatting. I couldn't hear their words but watched them light up the pipe and pass it around in a circle. The heavy-hipped woman stroked the attacked woman's head while the other one massaged her feet.

It occurred to me then that I hadn't been touched in a long time. The trees had touched me, and earth and water. But I hadn't had a human touch, warm hands—or even icy hands. No hands at all. I looked at mine. They were rough and awkward and dirty.

Thompie's touch had been most recent and probably the most soothing in my life. But since he deserted me, the memory of his touching left a rawness in my mouth—like metal or cold sores. Something you don't want to dwell on.

Before Thompie there was River Bill. But he rarely stroked me with the sort of kindness I witnessed as I watched those women. He touched me the same way he touched his new boat—glad to have it but touching it for his *own* pleasure. There was nothing in it for me.

Before River Bill, there'd been Mammie, who alternated between gentleness and violence. When I was small, her touches had reassured me. Sometimes during thunderstorms she scratched my back or rubbed my feet. Other times her wrath didn't spare me. I remembered the time a group of teenaged boys broke into her store and stole liquor, hitting her in the face again and again as she threatened to tell the police. When they'd gone, she beat me with her cane across my back as though I'd caused it. With Mammie's touching so unpredictable, it was hard to enjoy, much less anticipate.

And of course I was touched by the customers in her store. They would lead me out behind the bushes and press themselves into my mouth, their hands gripping my shoulders hard. And their touching haunted me so that I refused to think about it at all, refused to acknowledge it at all, dull, dull, dull, and it was gone.

I realized I'd never been touched, really. I'd been handled. There was a difference.

I imagined myself with those women, having them rub my back and stroke my legs. The thought ballooned in my chest until I found it hard to breathe.

The sun grew hotter, even in the thicket, and the fish I'd eaten earlier sat heavy in my stomach. My stomach felt swollen, and the infected cut burned as though I was pulling it apart with my fingers. I felt dizzy, and my mouth began sweating on the inside.

I hardly had time to sit up on my knees before my stomach emptied, loudly, and I heaved up water, and then just air. I coughed and spit and then felt the spasms hit again. Pressure built up in my temples until my head throbbed, and I gagged and coughed more, bringing up the hot remains of my breakfast. My head began to swim, and so I stretched back out on the ground and closed my eyes.

"Should one of us try to leave and get help?" a soft voice asked.

"I don't think so," answered another. "It's a good ten miles to the main road. Let's see how she's doing when she wakes up."

"I don't know, Caroline. She's going to need a lot more help than we can give her. She's got gashes all over, and . . .'' The voices faded out and in and out, and I couldn't understand them for a time, and I thought I might be underwater.

"Does that mean you're volunteering to walk out?"

"Yeah, I'll do it."

"Mariah can't leave. She knows first aid. It'll have to be one of us," the soft-spoken one replied.

I shifted my body and felt the covers above me rustle. The voices sounded very nearby, but when I opened my eyes, all I could see was grayness. I felt like I might be on a boat.

"I'm going to start boiling some water while you two work it out."

"I'll go," one of them said.

"No, I'll go. I don't mind."

"Why don't you both go. I'll stay here with her. It will be safer that way."

Then the voices elongated in my ears, and I couldn't make out the meaning anymore. I felt like I was being swallowed by the dark, although I couldn't tell if the darkness was wet or not, and since fighting suffocation feels just the same as suffocating, I gave in.

When I woke up again, the heavy-hipped woman with the braid was kneeling over me, wiping at my stomach with a hot cloth. I opened my eyes and let out a sigh.

"It's okay," she said. "I won't hurt you."

I looked at her face. She had round, blue, sparkly eyes with little lines extending from the corners.

"Sick," I told her. I could hear the word, but I wasn't sure it was the right one.

"I know," she said. "What's your name?"

"Don't-send-me-back," I managed.

"You need a doctor. Can you tell me your name?"

"Don't tell him—where I am," I begged. I wasn't sure I was saying what I meant to say. I couldn't tell where the sounds came from.

The woman dipped her cloth back into the bucket of water, then squeezed it out and wiped my face, slowly, so that I felt it pass over my eyelids and lips.

"My name's Mariah," she told me. "I was here camping with two of my friends. But you already know that, don't you?"

I nodded.

"Well, they've gone to get a doctor for you because you've been so sick. It might take a little while, but I won't leave you, okay?"

I nodded again.

"Can you tell me your name?"

"Jael."

"What?"

I pointed to my hip bone.

"Oh," she said.

"Don't let him touch me."

"Do you think you could drink a little juice? It might make you feel better."

And she reached her strong arm beneath my neck, lifting my head, and she held the tin mug of juice to my lips. I sipped it, and it was sweet.

The woman rubbed ointment into my cuts, and she

pulled the covers back over me and told me to sleep. Then she backed out of the tent, and I was alone.

I felt a heat warming my stomach, and when I opened my eyes, a thick red light was there, twirling like a tornado above my belly. The light disappeared into the cut place, and I felt it swirling and spinning around inside me and then leaking out between my legs like too much anger.

The thought of so much madness scared me, so I reached into myself to grab the red light. Instead, I pulled out my womb. It was shiny and pink and had never been touched before.

I reached again into myself and pulled out a second womb, a very old and weathered womb.

The light seemed to have disappeared, and my feet felt cold. I tugged the wombs onto my feet and wore them like shoes.

The next time I woke up, I couldn't remember where I was or where I was supposed to be. I threw the covers from around me, opened the tent flap and crawled out. It was night, and I saw a campfire, so I went to warm myself by it.

"Are you cold, Jael?" the woman asked.

"Who are you?" I answered.

"My name's Mariah, and I'm taking care of you until we can get you to a doctor."

"Oh," I replied, rubbing my hands together to warm them. "I'm cold."

"It's warm under the covers inside the tent," she told me.

"I don't like it in there."

"Can I bring the covers out to you, then?"

I nodded.

The woman walked away, and I stared into the sky. Lightning bugs flicked their bright lights off then on. I could see the moon and stars glowing like lightning bugs that never went off.

The woman returned and draped the blanket around my shoulders. I huddled beneath it.

"Do you want to rest your head in my lap?" she asked, and so I did.

"How are you feeling?"

"Good," I said. "No, not good, I mean."

"Your hair is the color of old maple leaves," she told me. "I like to touch it. It curls up around my fingers."

"Tangled."

"Yeah," she laughed. "It doesn't look like you've combed it in a while."

"Not here," I said.

"I need to put more medicine on your cuts."

So she opened my covers and leaned over me and dabbed the cream into my sore places on my stomach and thighs and arms. Her fat braid fell down beside my cheek, and I shifted my head to feel it tickle me there.

"Where did these cuts and scarred places come from?"

"Don't send me back."

"Did somebody cut you?"

"No, no," I tried to explain.

"Shhhh," she said.

After a time, Mariah picked up the bamboo flute and began to play a series of long, hollow notes. The music whispered something out to the darkness, and after that, I could hear nighttime whimpering empty.

"It's one of my favorite things," she said, catching her breath. "It's such nice music because it's so personal. No two people ever make the same sounds. It's like a fingerprint or a birthmark. Listen."

And she put the end of the flute to my ear and played, barely breathing, so that the music whistled like tingling air, and no one could hear it but me. The sound was beautiful and I felt clear-headed for a moment, almost lucid enough to know the rhythm of her breath.

"Thank you," I said.

But a loud puttering overhead kept Mariah from hearing me.

"It's a helicopter," she yelled. "We'll get on and go to the hospital."

I looked up into the sky to see bright lights descending on us. Mariah hugged me close to her as I watched the giant tadpole-shape land between our fire and the river.

They would not let the heavy-hipped woman come with me. I screamed and tried to run, telling them I had magic shoes, but I was barefoot. The medics strapped me down to a stretcher and explained that there was no other person around. Just before they took me away, I scanned the area with my eyes and saw nothing familiar. No Mariah, no tent. I couldn't even find the campfire.

Part Two

At first, I felt cold, and then the coldness rushed high into my head, drumming my heart's rhythm into my skull. The beat was steady, at least, and as long as I remained still and didn't try to open my eyes, I could concentrate only on the throbbing music and escape the pain.

I knew that there were people around. Their shoes periodically scuffed into the beat, clonked out of time, interrupting the pattern and sending me whirling into the pain again.

And then the drumming grew softer, more distant, as though the beats had been pounding me out, hammering me into some other form, and I was almost finished, my head newly shaped.

I woke up in a white room in a white bed with a brown, fake-wood footboard. Some people came in to speak with me, but I didn't look at them. I didn't want them to know my face. I didn't know it myself.

The doctors and nurses seemed skeptical of dirt, rinsing their hands at every opportunity, their white coats blowing behind them as they dashed in and out of the room. When they put their cold hands onto my skin, I shivered inside and pretended to be a leaf, falling slow from the top of a tall tree. Some days I was a maple. Or an oak, a birch, a dogwood, a prickly holly-tree leaf. I could float through the air for a long, long time without landing.

During the day, strangers would come in with clipboards tucked beneath white-jacketed arms, and taking turns, they'd question me. Some only wanted to know if I had insurance cards, next of kin, a Social Security number. Others offered me colored blocks and tested my knowledge of shapes. One man handed me a doll and told me to tie the shoes and button the jacket.

So much attention made my lips go dry. At first I ignored both the question and the questioner. But in time I discovered that they would leave me as soon as I gave them answers. I wasn't insulted by their questions or ridiculous requests. I didn't feel anything except slow.

The question they returned to again and again was simply, "Who *are* you?" I told them my name, and that was all.

"Can you remember *anything* else?" Dr. Sonthalia would ask me while she peered into the great gash in my middle. "Do you have *any idea* how you got these wounds?"

And I'd shake my head, staring at the hairs on my brown arms, peering into the freckles. Dr. Sonthalia's voice would drone on and on, and I'd answer her, I suppose, although in my mind, I was wishing I could lift the freckles from my body and collect them in a Mason jar. I wanted to shake them up and resprinkle them so they'd all have new neighbors. My plan was to concentrate them on my arms and face so that they'd be seen

every day and none would have to hide beneath my
hospital gown or sheet. And the great freckle sprinkler
who first decorated me would lose the pattern. Things
would surely change.

"This looks like some sort of ceremonial tattooing,
Jael. Do you remember any special gatherings, any cere-
monies?"

"No," I'd tell her absently, day after day, wondering
only if my freckles would come out if I sucked hard
enough. I knew they'd taste like cinnamon.

But after she left, I thought about her questions. In
the quiet between nurses and doctors and psychologists,
I'd peer beneath my sheets, beneath the hospital gown
at the scars sealing over on my legs, arms, breasts, and
stomach. I'd run my fingers along the peaked skin and
force myself not to open the healing places back up. The
large wound in the center was scabbing around the perimeter, and I continually yearned to pick at it, to capture
a bit of crust beneath my fingernail and to taste it. There
was nothing else to taste in the hospital. No appreciation
for flavors. But the wound was coated in a clear jelly and
covered by a thick gauze bandage. I convinced myself
that if I removed the bandage, the adhesive tape would
stretch and wrinkle and incriminate me before the
nurses.

I knew where I'd come from, at least in general
terms, and I knew very well that I didn't intend to go
back to River Bill. A vague notion of terror settled into
the muscles about my neck. And though I couldn't asso-
ciate the stiffness with anything in particular, I wore it
like a collar. It certainly had nothing to do with living in
the woods or on the river. I liked the woods and could

taste the river beneath my tongue. But I had a feeling that would not leave me, a feeling that shook my bowels and left me clammy. At the most unexpected times, it seemed like everything stopped inside my body—my blood no longer flowing, my kidneys refusing to separate fluids from wastes, my digestion shutting down, even my lungs seemed to hold their air as though it had congealed inside. It happened when I thought—about anything at all. And so I concentrated only on the curve of my fingernails and the ridges in my teeth.

"I'm so sorry," I kept saying, "I just can't remember." The social workers would try to hold my hands, but I wouldn't let them. I only cried once, and then I couldn't stop. I cried until exhaustion wrapped me like a shroud. And though the words were lies, the tears, I think, were real.

When all the missing-person checks were completed, when no one came to claim me, the social services department finally abandoned their search for my family. I was assigned a caseworker—a round and harmless woman named Helen Marston. Helen had light brown hair with no will of its own, falling straight down her back as though it were wet, and her bangs were very practical and short. At first, she tried to talk me into living in a halfway house with a bunch of other women, mostly former criminals. I argued that I didn't deserve to have criminals for roommates, but I didn't argue very well because I suspected that somehow Helen knew about Mammie's death even though I hadn't told. I thought of it as punishment. The only thing I knew for certain was that I didn't need punishing. We talked about my options for several days, and I insisted that I wanted to get a job and live alone—or have a room of my own at the very least.

"But you're not entirely socialized, Jael." Helen spoke with her eyes closed, her pudgy hand bracing her forehead.

"You're holding it against me—that I'm different from you," I claimed.

"It's just that a halfway house would give you a chance to learn to live with people. Group living has more advantages right now than going solo."

"I need some time to be alone," I told her. "How am I ever going to remember who I am if I'm always trying to protect myself from the convicts in the next bed?"

"I told you they aren't dangerous. Most of them were drug abusers—"

"Or child abusers," I added.

"They're being rehabilitated—the same as you."

Then Helen would get frustrated and move off to the window. I'd look down to my arms and blur my eyes until it seemed my freckles weren't freckles at all, but scabs. I'd look for freckles that overlapped follicles, never finding many, thinking only that freckles claim independence, demanding their own spaces.

"I'm not living in your halfway house," I told her. "There's no way."

The Mammie-ghost came to see me in the hospital. She was dirty and smelled like stale mud. At first I thought she was in a coffin, but then I realized it was a refrigerator. River Bill's refrigerator.

"What are you doing in the refrigerator?" I asked. "We buried you in a coffin. A metal one. I was there. You had a funeral and everything. You should stay where we buried you."

She dropped her mouth open like a squirrel hole, and worms started crawling out, crawling everywhere.

"Why'd you eat his bait?" I asked her. "I was supposed to sell those worms."

The bait dropped off her dress, down to the floor, and blindly started wiggling around.

"What are we supposed to fish with? How am I going to explain this to River Bill?"

My room smelled like swamp. The worms carpeted the place. Mammie was infested, and once again she'd brought her plagues to me.

"I loved you," I told her. "Why didn't you keep them away?"

She looked confused.

"I loved you," I cried. "Why do you keep doing this to me?"

She laughed and shook her head.

"Close your *mouth*," I yelled, and she was gone.

I tried not to befriend Helen. Lying to a friend was a difficult act. I knew I'd fail at it. But it was hard not to like her after she'd been around for a while. I liked the way her eyeshadow migrated up into wetly colored lines across her eyelids. I cherished her blinks. And then she'd smile back dumbly—thinking I was happy to see *her* and not just humored by her eye makeup.

One day Helen brought in a bag of clothes. As usual she was out of breath, complaining about the stairs and wiping perspiration from around her mouth.

"I know these probably aren't your style," she panted, "but I get tired of seeing you in those hospital gowns. So get up and get dressed."

I couldn't recall ever picking out clothes of my own. Clothes were only coverings, after all, and as long as they allowed me enough room to stretch and romp and kick, I didn't care about their designs. My clothes before had mostly been faded denim or solid cottons. So when I carried the bag into the bathroom and pulled out a white shirt with purple polka dots and a long red skirt, I could only think of clowns. Clowns in picture books and parades, using their clothes to disguise themselves. I started laughing when I realized I looked a little like Helen—wearing those clothes, all purple and red, because Helen's clothes always demanded attention and never exactly matched. I liked the skirt because it hung low and swished around my ankles. The wide elastic waistband didn't press too hard on my bandages.

Before I'd only worn skirts to church. Never at home. I decided I wasn't going to wear jeans ever again. I felt like someone else in skirts.

"You look exquisite," Helen told me as I reappeared.

"Thanks," I replied, feeling a little light-headed and made giddy by my new image.

"When they finally discharge you, we'll go over to the Goodwill together and you can pick out some things for yourself."

"I can't pay you for these," I admitted.

"You don't need to. They were donated."

But the clothes seemed new.

I sat down in the chair beside the bed, still a little weak but not wanting to be a patient anymore. Helen kicked off her shoes and sat down on the bed, pulling her fleshy legs up beneath her.

"You ever been fishing?" I asked her.

"Not since I was a kid."

"I'll take you sometime."

As soon as the words left my mouth, I expected Helen to start quizzing me about fishing. But Helen seemed to miss the reference, gazing off in silence, like she had something on her mind.

"Listen, Jael," she finally said. "I probably shouldn't tell you this, but I think I might have found you a job."

"Where?"

"Now, don't get excited over it yet. I'll still have to talk this over with the committee, and they're going to want to put you in that halfway house. But I spoke with a friend of mine, Arthur, and told him about your situation. He's the priest at a church just outside the city. Anyway, he said that they'd just lost their custodian, and they might be able to use you."

"What do I have to do?" I asked her desperately, wadding up my skirt in my hands.

"It isn't settled yet, so don't get your hopes up. *If* this goes through, you'd be dusting, polishing the railings, sweeping the steps. I'm pretty sure they hire a cleaning service to come in for the hard stuff."

"When would I be able to start?"

Helen caught the enthusiasm in my voice and cast me an amused glance, throwing up her hands like I was about to attack. "Slow down," she said. "I still have to work out the details, and I think we probably shouldn't spend much time talking about it until I see how receptive the committee is."

"But where would I live?"

Helen laughed.

"The woman who left the job lived with her family somewhere nearby, but Arthur mentioned an old apartment in the basement of the church. He said it hadn't been opened up in years, so he doesn't know what condition it's in. We don't need to worry about living arrangements just yet, though."

Living in a church. The whole concept struck me as odd in a funny way, a way that made me uncomfortable but also seemed like destiny. When I had slept in the church years earlier as a child, I remembered finding a birthmark that I'd never noticed before on the bottom of my foot. I checked to make certain the pea-sized purple speckle still existed.

"A church would suit me fine," I told Helen, stroking the arch of my foot. "The Lord knows me well."

"Really? Did you remember something? Are you having a memory?"

For a moment, I imagined telling her about my relationship to churches. What would she think, I wondered, if I said I'd been a deacon's daughter? Or wife?

I decided against it—not sure of my phrasing.

In the hospital, it hadn't occurred to me that a whole city sprawled out from every direction. On my first day out, I was awe-struck, scared, and partially frozen by that slow anxiety that had made its home in me.

The city was bigger than anywhere I'd ever been. All the stoplights and traffic and car horns and businesses and signs and restaurants made my head spin with a tornado's vengeance. It seemed like the clutter had me surrounded. We drove and drove and never seemed to leave it. I realized that Helen had probably been right when she'd suggested the halfway house. I had no idea how to live in so much action. It was like an aggravated ant colony, seething and teeming with motion.

Helen followed the highway for a long time, driving on a road that went beneath another road, and I could see the third and fourth roads jutting out at funny angles all around us. It seemed like we were going really fast and driving on a structure way up in the air where no human ought to be comfortable. When Helen got off the highway, she turned down a side road and then down another road until we came to a neighborhood with big grassy lawns and trees. I found it a little easier to breathe, but my stomach still spasmed at the thought of being so lost. For a second, I even wished for the bare and clinical safety of the hospital.

I had no idea which direction the river was in.

At an intersection, Helen turned into a long driveway. I could see the great stone building up ahead, with turrets and steeples and large arches in the doorways.

"This is it," Helen said.

It was like no church I had seen before.

She drove all the way through the parking lot and onto the grass at the back of the giant structure. Pulling her car up next to a small set of steps that descended to a doorway below ground level, she parked and called out, "Come on."

Helen opened her door, and so I followed even though I felt the pressure of a hundred hands grabbing at my throat.

"Home, sweet home," Helen mumbled as she opened the door. The musky odor of the underground greeted me, and I stepped inside.

I looked around at the stone walls and exposed beams, the dust padding the hardwood floor. In the center of the high ceiling was a single lightbulb with a cord hanging down. When I pulled it, I saw that the place was coated in dust and spiderwebs.

"Pretty filthy right now," Helen said. "But you can probably get it cleaned up this afternoon. I brought loads of supplies."

She left the door open so the apartment could air out while I worked, telling me that she'd return before night to take me back to the hospital where I was staying until my apartment and job were ready.

I didn't start cleaning right away. From the door-steps I watched Helen drive off, and even after she had gone, I sat on the steps and rubbed my hands in the dirt.

Next, I explored—running my hands along the old and soft-edged stones that made up my walls. There was a tiny, narrow fireplace, and its high, arched opening reminded me that I was in a church. Above, a thick mantel rested on the stones, its wood dark and shiny beneath the dust.

The beams in the ceiling and at each corner of the room looked like small versions of railroad ties. Spider-webs dangled from the beams. "Sweep out those cobwebs," Helen had said. But I understood the spiders—their tender art too personal for light places, their boneless bodies protected by nothing but the stillness of that space. I decided to let them stay.

Behind a wide and heavy door, I discovered a closet. It was so large and deep that it had its own lightbulb. Inside, I found a bar long enough to hold more hanging clothes than I'd ever own. There was also a chest of drawers, dusty and empty, and a high shelf. Against the back wall, I found another door. When I unbolted and opened it wide, I saw that it opened into a dim hallway. And when I squinted my eyes, I could see other doors with numbers lining the corridor.

Quickly, I closed that door, blocking the great church off from my space, and returned to the apartment. The refrigerator in the far corner looked too old to work. But when I touched it, I felt the coolness and noted its hum. Inside it was empty and dirty.

Off to the side of the apartment was a miniature door. It was so short I had to stoop to keep from bumping my head on the doorframe, and inside, I found the bathroom. It could have been designed for a child. The toilet sat low to the ground—like the ones at the school I attended when I was very small. The sink stood level with my hips and the bathtub was far too short for any adult to stretch out in. Somehow the shrunken proportions excited me—made me feel as if I'd wandered into a fairy tale. I checked the water. It ran rusty for a while, but then a clearness came. The tiny stream trickled across the sink's porcelain base and cut through the dirt that had settled.

It seemed wisest to clean the walls first, so I ran water

in my bucket, added cleaning fluid that smelled like pine sap, and proceeded to wipe down the rough stones. They shredded my sponges, ate holes right through their centers, and I started thinking about how good it would feel to have power to scrape away soft layers. As I cleaned, I made a list of the objects I'd scrape if I were a stone. Skin, I thought. I'd scrape people—one layer at a time until rawness set in and forced them to remember that they were alive. To remember that they were alive and not so durable.

As I worked, I scraped the skin off my own hands, and I marked those stones with bits of soft tissue, claiming them with the fine, curling remnants of cells.

While I was scrubbing the wall, I found a hole. Low, near the corner of one wall, was a place where the mortar between two stones had broken and chipped away, leaving an opening a little larger than an ear. I stuck two fingers in the hole and then the handle of a broom. It went all the way through, into a dark place. I plugged it up with a shredded sponge and continued cleaning.

As I sat on the hearth, waiting for the floor to dry and resting my sore body, I questioned myself for taking such pains to wipe the grime from cracks in the floorboards. I didn't mind dirt. Never had. I ate the bland picnic lunch the cafeteria had made for me.

I went into the bathroom and sprinkled the green disinfectant and cleanser onto the porcelain. Above the sink, I found a small mirror, and I looked at myself for a minute. My face was so thin that the bones protruded. Beneath my cheeks, my face looked almost hollow. The eyes that I remembered being brown seemed yellow.

At least my hair was okay, I thought, the same deep

brown as always, thick and long and not showing the knot that had tightened at the base of my neck. I wondered how I was going to get it out.

I cleaned the closet, dusting out each drawer in the bureau and wiping down all the baseboards.

When I could think of nothing else to do, I scrubbed out the refrigerator, plucking carcasses of bugs from the tray beneath the freezer.

I didn't know what time it was or how long it would be before Helen returned. So I wandered around outside, wanting to explore the wooded area behind the church but deciding that there'd be time to investigate later. I only allowed myself to explore the edge, but even there, I found treasures: a heavy stick and a small sharp rock.

On the cool concrete doorsteps in the oak tree shade, I whittled out the remainder of my afternoon in the wooden face of a hag.

On the day that Arthur gave me a tour of the church, I started bleeding. I couldn't remember how much time had passed since I'd last felt that warmth pass out of me. I'd forgotten how slow the pain came, how the fistlike tightness released and tightened again, how low the ache.

We walked through the sanctuary together, and Arthur showed me the great frames on the walls that had to be wiped clean. He led me through the labyrinth of pews, reminding me to take the songbooks and little magazines out before spraying greasy polish on the narrow book-holders. He lifted a balled-up silver gum wrapper from the floor and slipped it into his pocket.

Behind the main altar, he showed me canisters of holy water and regular water. He pointed out that the large silver bowl in the foyer would need shining before Sunday.

Arthur was a surprise to me. He stood shorter than I did, and his body was thin and stooped. Because he was Helen's friend, I'd expected him to be close to her age, but he was weathered, his skin slipping off the bones in a way that made me want to poke it and watch it jiggle. I imagined it'd feel like biscuit dough. Age seemed to have softened his tongue.

He was about the same age as River Bill.

I'd asked Helen what I should call her friend, and she told me to call him Father. I decided not to call him anything at all.

He was leading me down a side aisle when we passed an ornate structure of little closets that could have been playhouses, their wooden doors decorated with curvy designs, chiseled and smooth. I didn't know what could be inside such tiny rooms. They intrigued me. I wondered if I'd need to go inside to clean, from time to time.

I stopped walking to examine them closer although Arthur continued down the aisle. The booths had been painted a deep green, but an overcoat of gold gave them the gilded look of royalty. They looked like they belonged in a castle. I ran my finger along a diamond pattern cut into the wood.

"Father," I called. And when he turned to look at me, I blushed and turned my eyes to the old wooden floor.

"Oh, yes," he said absently. "The confessionals. Yes, I'm glad you reminded me."

He scurried my way, removed a key from his pocket and proceeded to open the center door. Inside, a sturdy red velvet chair on wheels spanned the width of the space. The walls on either side had opaque screens supported by narrow ironwork grilles.

"You'll need to—" He faltered and then closed the door. "You can just wipe things down every month or so."

I grabbed on to the corner of the confessional as I felt a sudden, doubling ache and then a warm dripping between my legs. I could feel it spilling onto my underwear, staining flowers.

Arthur opened up the smaller door to the right of the central one, and I saw that the little room had nothing inside but a kneeling bench covered in the same rich velvet. More than anything else, I wanted to kneel, to collapse into myself, into the pain, and let that dark space hold me like a womb.

He shut the little door and laughed, "Once a month should do it. Nobody stays in there long enough to dirty them up. Of course the air needs fumigating."

I pretended to understand and laughed weakly.

From there he led me to the back of the sanctuary and down another hallway to the supply closet. A faintness came over me when he opened the door and the smells of disinfectants seeped into my lungs. Something seized my belly then, something inside, invisible, squeezing. I placed my hands on my lower back to keep myself steady.

"Here you have your basic cleaning solutions," Ar-

thur began, lifting up a toilet-bowl brush for me to examine. "There should be enough here to get us through
the winter. If we run low on something, let me know."

Arthur spoke with me about architecture, about
stained glass, about the benefits of marble and the
shortcomings of vaulted ceilings. We were standing in
the shrine of Mary, Holy Virgin, when Arthur glanced
at his watch, let out a little hoot, and said, "Forgive
me, Jael, but I've got to leave." And he started walking
away, looking behind and saying, "Make yourself comfortable. Poke around. You can start working tomorrow."

I watched as the little black suit whizzed down the
aisle and out the front door. Arthur had a friskiness
about him that I could appreciate, but he didn't act like
the religious men I'd known.

Around me I could smell the metallic aroma of
blood, and I thought of Mammie's head, coppery and
wet. I looked to the Madonna, her scalp solid, unchip-
pable, immortal—the way a mother's head should be. In
my mind, I heard a voice telling me to paint her robe
with my redness. It seemed to come from the Virgin
herself. If so, I disobeyed.

In early autumn I slept with the door open, chilly but
welcoming the first rays of day as they edged their way
into my cave and across my eyelids. From my bed, I
could see the woods behind the church, the kudzu vines
strapped tight around the trees as though they were
holding slaves captive.

In the daytime, I locked my door and entered the church from the inside.

Mornings, when the earliest light shone through the stained-glass windows and cast its silvery dimness on the high, pale walls, I made my rounds through the church, nodding to greet the stone statues who lived in separate, private domes on the perimeter of the sanctuary. Two or three of the men I could not keep straight—either Peter, Paul, or Pius—but their sculpted holiness jutted from the white. At the altar of Christ, I stopped to straighten the row of chairs, aligning them like broken bones, crooked teeth, seashells washed up on the same spent wave.

The Madonna's altar was the only one with a wheel-chair ramp. Naturally, she was my favorite. She was the first woman that I loved.

Each morning I bathed her first, privately, pretend-ing that she was my own mother and that her modesty required my immediate attention. I crept into the church early enough that my lungs were still flavored with night, and I filled a silver chalice with holy water, dabbing at her face gently with gauze and never letting my fingers graze her smooth stone skin. I had to stand on a stepladder to reach her large eyes. I wiped her eyelids with a cotton swab, tracing indentations.

I didn't know the rules for cleaning statues, but it seemed to me only appropriate to refrain from using chemicals or polishes on the Virgin. I sponged her robe meticulously, checking each day for stains. She was dust-repellent. She glowed, snowy as milk.

I saved the Virgin's bathwater, carrying it back with me to the supply closet. In the darkness between the

brooms and brushes, beneath the high shelf stocked
with paper towels and toilet tissue, I drank that water
like nectar. It made me light-headed each time.

Arthur had a habit of leaving notes for me in the
supply closet. He was a busy man, always attending to
business as well as souls. I only saw him occasionally,
but his correspondence kept me up to date about which
duties to perform on what day.

One December morning, I bundled into my clothes
and headed out through my closet along the back corri-
dors and up the chilly stairwell. On the supply room
door, I found Arthur's letter:

> Dear Jael,
>
> Please take the dirty clothes to the Laun-
> dromat and wash them. Don't put anything
> delicate in the machines. You can do the
> lace things by hand and hang them in a
> classroom. Take your time.
>
> Construction workers will be in and out
> of the church for a while. Don't let them
> bother you. You may have to sweep after
> they leave. I'll be away until tomorrow night.
>
> You're an angel.
>
> Father Burke

I decided to let Jesus, Paul, Peter, and Pius wait to
have their altars cleaned, and so after sponging off the

Virgin, I collected all the table covers and altar clothes that wouldn't shred in the washing machine.

The Laundromat was only a couple of blocks away, but the heavy basket of linens made the walk seem longer. My arms shook as I walked down the quiet street. Even though it was December, I was sweating beneath my long, hooded sweater.

Inside, the heat from the dryers turned the Laundromat into a steam bath. I filled the washers quickly, and then stepped outside to give my lungs a chance to know the air.

Engraved into the stone above the building was the single word "Manuel." I'd looked at the word many times, finding it peculiar, the cold block letters sunk deep into the rock. As I stared up at the word again, wondering if it should read "manual" instead of "Manuel," I heard a loud and childish voice behind me say "Hey."

I turned to see a rumpled woman of forty or more, standing nearby and looking up at the sign as well.

"Name of the Lord," she said, thick-tongued and slurring. Her hair was short and black and curled up on the ends. Her body was swollen and fleshy, and she wore a thin floral housedress only one layer thicker than her skin.

"What?"

"Name of the Lord. Manuel. Name of the Lord," she repeated. Her voice jerked high, almost like a yodel.

I smiled at her and went inside to check my clothes. The woman followed me in but was distracted by a man standing by the vending machines, getting a cup of coffee.

"Hey," she said, sounding so loud and friendly that I thought she must know him. Then I saw discomfort flicker across his face like a private itch. "I'm cold," the woman continued. "If I had fifty cents, I could get some coffee."

The man didn't respond to her, didn't even acknowledge her, but the woman persisted. "So cold," she added, and stuck her palm out like a small child.

The lights went off on each of my four washers, and one by one, I emptied them, tossing the holy rags into the great, hot dryers. I cast a glance out the window where the coldness made the air look dingy. I was sweating again.

The strange woman was sitting in a hard plastic chair by the window, looking down at her well-worn tennis shoes. Her face was soft, so soft, in fact, that I was certain she could punch her lead tongue right through her cheek if she tried. I worried that she didn't take raindrops seriously enough.

Without meaning to, I caught her eye. Instantly, she was up and heading my way.

"I'm hot," she said. "If I had fifty cents, I could get a Coke."

I reached into my pocket and fished out the change. It had come from a collection plate, after all. I didn't know the church doctrine, but I knew that feeding the poor was always implied.

She took the change and then looked at me and asked, "You mad?"

"Mad?" I questioned. "At you?"

"I'm sorry," she whispered, and I thought she might cry, her chin lifting up into her mouth space. I could see perspiration outlining her hairline, and my instinct was to lap it up.

"I'm not mad at all," I told her.

She dropped the money into the drink machine and turned back to me for approval just before she pressed the grape juice button.

Later, while I was folding the white things, she took my hand and pulled me to the far corner of the Laundromat where all the washers' hoses emptied into a soapy hole in the floor.

"See it bubble." She pointed. "Men pee-pee there. In the bubbles. I like to drink it."

While she helped me finish my laundry, I noticed her shriveled fingers and her dry, shrimplike lips. I liked her because she had grape juice all around her mouth and because she honored trenches and wet places and tried not to make people angry. Later I knew she wouldn't recognize me, so I gave her a holy cloth to keep and told her to wipe her face.

When I returned to the church, I saw that the big front door was propped open, and a beat-up station wagon was backed up to the high concrete steps. From the back end of the car, long pieces of wood jutted out.

I carried my basket into the church only to hear the grating shrillness of a saw coming from the coatroom adjacent to the foyer. I wasn't religious, but I'd grown to respect the home of the stone family, rimming the main altar like guardians. I didn't like to witness the violation of their quiet.

As I polished the brass candleholders, I heard the saw start and stop, again and again. Then the carpenter sneezed and continued his cutting. The sneeze was hard, and I imagined him fat and bearded, his pants slid low on his hips, his shirt pulling away to reveal a hint of inconsistent hairiness on his lower back.

I hated the places on men's bodies that couldn't decide whether or not to grow hair.

I spit on my cloth and buffed those hard stands until the shine reflected the tiniest mole on my chin.

I saved the brass railings out front for last. It was cold, and the blue liquid I sprayed onto the railings seeped through my cloth and wet my hands icy. With one hand in my pocket and the other polishing as quickly as I could, I watched the carpenter walk out of the door carrying scrap wood.

"How do you do?" he asked and moved to his car.

I nodded and changed hands.

He was thin and wore only jeans, boots, and a flannel shirt with the sleeves rolled up. He picked up another piece of wood and, seemingly unaffected by the brisk weather, he headed back up the steps and into the church. As he passed by, I looked at his long arms, muscular but narrow. I finished my job and followed along.

I was halfway up the aisle when I heard him call. "Miss?"

I turned around.

"Do you work here?"

With my brass cleaner in one hand and assorted rags dangling from the other, I rolled my eyes and nodded. He laughed.

"You don't know, by any chance, where I could get a broom, do you?"

So he followed me back to the supply room.

"I'm Wallace Mulhern," he said. "Been hired out for a pretty big job here. I guess you'll be seeing a lot of me."

Though he sounded friendly enough, I saw no reason to entertain him. I nodded.

"I meant to bring my own broom, but I forgot it. I appreciate you letting me use yours."

We reached the closet, and for an instant, an old familiar terror washed over me. "You stay out here," I told him.

Quickly I flicked on the light switch, grabbed the broom and dustpan, and made it back outside. Wallace stood just where I'd left him.

"Hey, did I do something to make you uncomfortable?" he asked.

"Not really."

"Because if I did, I didn't mean it."

We headed back into the sanctuary in silence.

"No kidding. I'm just doing my job. I made a mess, and I wanted to clean it up."

"That's *my* job," I told him.

"Okay," he said.

Wallace picked up pieces of wood while I swept sawdust. He was older than I'd thought at first, and he had dark hair that fell straight down into his collar. I noticed lines forking out from the corners of his eyes, wondered if they were replications of his palm—tiny heart, head, and life lines that shifted with each blink. I began to suspect he carried an ancient soul, though he teased like someone younger.

"Aren't you going to tell me what I did that bugged you so much?"

"No."

"If you don't tell me, how do you know I won't do it again tomorrow?"

"You will."

"Not if you tell me what not to do."

I emptied my dustpan into the garbage. "You just make a lot of noise. With all that sawing and hammering. You shouldn't do that here."

Wallace paused a moment, and I thought I might have hurt his feelings. Then he asked, "You don't ever have to vacuum this place, do you?"

"That's different," I said, but I was blushing. Noise was noise and excuses were excuses, and Wallace had caught me in one. I continued my confused argument anyway. "The vacuum keeps the floors clean. It's a constructive noise."

"More constructive, say, than building new confessionals? More constructive than *building* something for Christ?" He cocked his head and looked at me seriously, but I could see play in his half-winked eyes.

"Okay, okay, I give up," and I laughed because he was smiling, and because he was sarcastic, and because we'd become friends, already, by accident. "Really, though, it seems odd that you'd build them inside."

"Easier that way. They weigh a lot. It'd be a task to get them up the church steps and through the doors without skinning the woodwork."

Wallace held the dustpan, and I swept the remnants of wood into it. The sawdust got in his nose, and he scrunched up his face in an almost-sneeze.

"Think about cow's tits," I said, and was immediately embarrassed.

"What?"

"Cow's tits," I answered shyly. "Think about them when you have to sneeze, and it will go away."

He laughed, sneezed anyway, pulled a bandana out of his jeans pocket, and wiped his nose.

"Where'd you say you come from?" he asked.

"I didn't."

I made one last attempt at getting the smallest particles into the pan, and Wallace dumped it into the garbage. I noticed that he'd thrown lots of triangles and squares of wood into the trash.

"Are you throwing away those little pieces?"

"Yeah. They're not big enough to use."

"Would it be okay if I took a couple with me?" I asked him. "I like to whittle."

"Really?" He sounded interested. "What kind of knife do you use?"

"Just a regular kitchen knife," I told him. "Is that okay?" I felt young and dumb for having mentioned whittling in the first place. Obviously I was supposed to have a special knife.

"Hmmm," Wallace said. "I've never whittled with a kitchen knife before. I usually use a pocketknife. Do kitchen knives work?"

"Sort of. I used to have a pocketknife, but I lost it," I lied. "I don't know if a kitchen knife works as well."

"I do some carvings of my own. I'll show you some-time if you want. Don't live too far away."

"That'd be good, I guess." I felt a little dizzy. I hadn't had much practice with conversations.

Wallace rummaged through the garbage. "This piece might be good," he said and handed it to me.

My apartment was sparsely furnished—a bed, a table, a cabinet, a small heater, a chair that rocked and one that didn't. I liked the open space and preferred the floor to furniture. So that night after soaking my bones in the tub and then wrapping myself in a blanket, I sat against the wall and chipped away at the wooden block Wallace had given me. I had no particular figure in mind and found myself admiring the thin slivers littering my floor as much as the block itself.

While I worked, I heard footsteps entering the adja-cent room, a classroom in the church. I heard the scrap-ing of chairs along the floor and muffled voices. I'd never known anyone to use that room on a weeknight.

I went to the door and peered out to see if other people were milling around. The night was blustery, and the naked limbs of the oak tree outside my door clicked together and creaked. Seeing no one, I went back in.

No other noises distracted me as I heated soup, ate, and then washed my dishes. But when I bent to put the bowl away, I heard a voice again. I knelt beside the wall and tried to listen.

That's when I remembered the hole between the

stones. Quietly I pulled the old sponge from its crevice. When I peeked through the hole, I could see feet, lots of feet dangling from chairs. The voices were too dim to distinguish between words. So I crawled over to the space heater and unplugged it. Then I stretched out, belly down, and peeking through the hole, strained to hear the speaker's words.

"Another *fucking* dream," she said. "Just when I think I've dealt with everything, I have another fucking dream. This time I was swimming in the ocean, and when I tried to come up for air, a *big* fucking hand pushed my head back down. And no matter where I swam, the hand was there, and I couldn't breathe. And then I woke up.

"I don't know what it means." And she paused.

Nobody spoke, and I lay there stiffly, scared that if I moved someone would hear me, catch me intruding— on what, I didn't know.

"Of course I know what it means," she admitted. This time she was crying and I could hear the rumbling anger in her throat. "It *means* that I'm *still* not over it. It means that at least in my sleep, I'm still vulnerable to *him*. Goddamn him."

I did not know what sort of situation would cause a woman to curse so freely in a safe and holy place. I wondered if the place was holy to her. I wondered why no one else spoke. The taste of blood spread through my mouth, and I realized I'd bitten away the inside of my lower lip.

"I'm glad to be here," the woman said, her voice strong again. "I'm glad we have this new place to meet.

It feels a lot safer to me. Thanks for listening, and I pass."

Again there was silence, and when another person started speaking, I plugged up the wall.

When I went to bed that night, I couldn't sleep. Each time I closed my eyes, I pictured Mammie's store and saw myself wandering through the maze of pool tables, eye-level to the zippers on the pants of grown men. Bumping into zippers, their zippers against my nose, the slow and deliberate sound of a zipper edging down, the quick zip as fingers yanked it up.

There was enough room in my closet for the bed, and so I moved it there, tugging and pushing until I'd secured my place. I made myself think about Wallace, about what I should carve into his piece of wood. Something holy, I thought. Something magic.

"Jael," she whispered, "come out."

At first I thought it was the wind that woke me up, whistling through the cracks in the bark of the oak tree. But I kept hearing my name.

I sat up in my bed, strained my ears, and listened for the voice again.

I cracked open the closet door and peeked out into the apartment. No one was there.

Outside the window, I could see the shadows of low limbs waving in the night air.

"The moon," she called again. "Come look at the moon."

I recognized the voice but couldn't remember where I'd heard it before. It sent chills through my backbone. I felt haunted. Without turning on the light, I pulled on my long hooded sweater and shoes. Then I sat on the hearth and listened to see if she'd continue to speak.

Again, she called, "Jael."

She was outside my door, the woman from the Laundromat. She crouched beside the church, and in the outside light, her dark eyes peered up at me like polished eightballs. She had the holy cloth tied around her head like a scarf.

"You almost missed it," she said thickly.

"Missed what?"

"Night. Come see the moon."

The woman led me deep into the woods. The trees were old and wide, but since their leaves had fallen, they didn't block the sky. Their light limbs spread across the sky like veins.

The land was familiar to me for a while, and then we came to a tangle of briers. I'd avoided the briers before, but the woman plowed through as though she didn't feel them tearing at her skin. Though they caught in my sweater and scratched my legs and face, I followed along.

Past the briers, crape myrtles sprang up, knobby-trunked and rustling. A stream glistened just below the trees. The woman grabbed my arm and pulled me beneath the limbs down to the side of the stream.

We sat, side by side, and watched the moon's reflection ripple and waver. I was shivering, but the woman didn't seem affected by the cold. She was wearing the same summer dress I'd seen her in earlier. She didn't even have a jacket.

After a while, I began to wonder how she'd found me, how she knew who I was, and why she'd pulled me out of my bed that night. So I asked her name.

"Mariah," she told me.

"What?" I asked, confused and thinking I'd misheard.

"Madonna," she said. But her words came out so tongue-laden that I still wasn't sure I'd heard her correctly.

"Who?"

"Magdelena," she yelled, laughing. "Come."

The woman jumped up and started peeling off her clothes. Then she stepped into the stream, knelt down, and lapped at the surface like an animal. From the trees, I watched her move. She was fat-padded and lusty in the way she swayed in the water.

"You come," she called. "Get wet."

"It's cold," I protested.

"Not under the moon," she slurred. "Get under the moon. Not under the man." And she cackled aloud to herself.

Reluctantly, I shed my clothes, and even as I undressed, I was unsure why I was doing it. I hung my things from the branches of a crape myrtle and waded out.

The stream was icy, and at first, I stood statue-like.

"Yes, yes, under the moon."

"Under the moon," I repeated through chattering teeth.

She spun around in a circle and motioned me to do

the same. Soon I was spinning giddy with her. Together we watched the moon glowing, that brilliant circle of light, and I grew so woozy I felt warm.

We rubbed our bodies in mud and plastered crinkly, dry leaves to our skin. Amid the crape myrtles, we darted and laughed and rolled until I grew tired and slept.

At some point, I heard her say, "Have to go now."

" 'Bye," I called back, dream-dulled.

And when I woke up later, I found the altar cloth spread across my body.

At the edge of the woods, I stood, clothes draped over my mud-crusted arm, confused and staring at the closed door to my apartment. I couldn't decide whether to dress myself and soil my clothes or run naked for the door and wear the clothes again when I was clean.

I looked around and saw only Wallace's parked station wagon. Around me the morning was wet, and though I could see my breath clabbering in the air, only my feet were cold. If Wallace was already working, I realized I must be late.

I bolted out of the woods, my body cloaked in earth, the dry leaves blowing from my hair. As I approached the concrete steps, I heard a crackling and turned to see Wallace shuffling through the leaves.

By the time he saw me, I was already descending the steps. I didn't catch his expression.

My tiny bathtub turned into a river, and I rinsed my clumpy, tangled hair in the brown water around me.

Little sticks and pieces of leaves floated on the surface.
It felt familiar. I didn't drain the tub.

Behind the Virgin Mary, there was a wall-sized picture made of glass. In the picture, a blue-clad Mary held
the diapered Baby Jesus in her arms. His baby hands
reached up to play with her ear.

I closed my eyes and imagined the graze of tiny
fingers against the rim of my earlobe.

"Mosaic," Wallace said, and I jumped. I hadn't
known he was there. I knew how to walk without being
heard, but I didn't trust others with the same soft-soled
ability.

"What?" I asked, then blushed. I hadn't spoken with
Wallace at all since he'd seen me running naked. On the
first day, we'd avoided each other. The second day I
stayed far from his workplace, washing down the chalk-
boards in classrooms and scrubbing baseboards in the
bathrooms. By the third day, I knew I had to return to
the sanctuary. The statues hadn't been bathed. The
marble ledges needed wiping.

"It's a mosaic," he said. "Little tiny pieces of
painted glass and marble all fit together to make the
design."

"Oh."

"Probably five hundred years old, that piece. Took
somebody a whole lifetime to put it together."

Wallace stared up at the picture, turning his head
slowly from side to side. If I hadn't known his appreciation for that piece, for that artist, I would have surely

thought he was worshipping the Virgin like so many old women who tilted their heads the same way as they passed through the church on weekdays. Wallace carried a peculiar smell—like winter sweat and tree sap. When I looked at his face, I was surprised, again, by the depth of those wrinkles around his eyes. He was chewing gum, and I watched his strong jaw.

"I'm getting ready to leave for the day," he told me. "I wanted to apologize—about the other morning."

His warm voice steamed the air around me. I could feel my eyes getting moist, though I wasn't sure why. How far, I wondered, would my tongue sink into those wrinkles?

"I'm pretty embarrassed too," he said. "I don't know whether you know it or not, but I was, uhm, looking for a bush. I'd been drinking a lot of coffee."

Wallace broke into a grin, and though I didn't really believe him, I caught myself laughing. The laugh came up surprisingly from my belly. It reminded me of the times when Mammie would wring a chicken's neck, and I'd watch it flop around on the ground, desperate and in circles. My laugh came out like those flapping wings, and when it subsided, I felt relieved.

"No hard feelings?"

"No hard feelings," I repeated.

"In that case," he said, "why don't you come take a look at what I've been working on? I need an objective opinion." He jabbed me gently on the arm and led the way down the aisle back to the coatroom where he'd set up a workshop.

Inside, he picked up a piece of wood, about the length of my arm, that curved in and out.

"I've been working on the balusters. They're the hardest part."

"The hardest part of what?"

"Of the confessionals."

I looked around the room to see the closetlike boxes in progress, but found only a variety of balusters in different sizes.

"Where are they?" I asked.

"What?"

"The confessionals that you're building?"

"Right here," and he pointed to the balusters again, his eyes squinting as he smiled. "Actually, constructing the room is the easiest part. It's the details that take longest."

"What are the—the balusters for?"

"Usually they support railings, like on staircases. But here they're just decoration. When it's finished, they'll be lined up against the top—like bars on a window."

I thought of the scars on my body, the little intricate ones that had taken hours and the crude ones that I'd slashed rashly. I thought about details, carved lovingly and planned.

I thought about jail.

In my hand, I held a small baluster and stroked its perfect smoothness with my thumb.

"Jael?" I heard him call. "Can you come play now?"

"Huh?"

"My mommy said I could ask you to play."

Even after I opened my eyes, I couldn't see the little

boy. My long sweater and skirts hung down over my face. But I could feel him sitting on my toes. He reached up to my knees and tapped them lightly, back and forth.

"Jael," he whined, "get up."

I pushed away the clothes obscuring my view, and there he was, Baby Jesus, dressed in a clean white T-shirt and a cloth diaper. He had cheeks the color of persimmons.

He climbed up my body until he had straddled my waist. Then he reached up and brushed my cheek and said, "Don't cry."

I hadn't known I was crying.

He led me from my room into the woods, his little fat legs crawling and pointing.

Once, he tripped over a stick.

When we got to a hollow tree, he took my hand and pulled me through the bark. I could feel the tree caressing my face, and it made me tingle.

Inside the tree, there was room for us to sit on the ground cross-legged and talk.

"Want some tea?" Jesus asked.

"Sure," I told him.

And he handed me a wooden mug filled with a sweet liquid that burned its way down my throat and made me shiver.

"I skinned my knees," he said. "Will you kiss them?"

And so I kissed his tiny round legs and licked away the blood. Beneath my tongue, his scraped little body healed like a hope.

"You're magic," he said.

"Not *me*," I argued.

"Uh-huh," he insisted. "You just don't know it yet."

I considered his words, his odd charm, his funny hands.

"I love bark," he said. "The nicest thing about bark is you can flake it into pieces and it turns right back into earth again. See?" And he began breaking the bark between his fingers. When he looked up again, he asked, "Do you like to climb trees?"

"Sure," I said.

"Me too. Come on."

I followed him up the tree for a time, and even though he was small, he ascended with cat-speed. "Smells good, doesn't it?" he called from above.

I sniffed the tree wall, and it smelled musky, like a closet or an attic. I ran my hands along the side of the tree, scaling up behind Jesus. When I looked to see how high he had climbed, I watched his white bottom move out of sight.

"Baby Jesus?"

"You have to believe you can make it," he called back, "or you'll fall." But he called from a long way away—so far away that I could hardly hear. Then I wasn't sure I'd heard him at all.

"Baby Jesus?"

He didn't answer me. The bark became slick. There were no ledges for my toes to curl around, and I began to slip.

I found myself alone, stroking the cool stone wall behind my bed.

~~~

"The first one's together," Wallace yelled.

I was up at the main altar, polishing the railing on the winding staircase that led up to a platform where Arthur spoke to his churchgoers.

"What?" I yelled back. There was no one in the church but us, so it didn't matter if we made noise. Earlier, one man had come to pay homage to a saint, and we'd shut up. But he left after twenty minutes or so, and Wallace started reciting passages again from a play I'd never heard of in a funny dialect I couldn't even recognize. We called jokes back and forth to one another for the rest of the morning.

"I said the first one's done. Come see it."

So I stopped where I was, leaving my dusty cloth and the furniture polish on the red carpeted steps, and hurried down the aisle to the coatroom.

Wallace stood proudly beside the tall boxlike structure that bore the ornate markings of a confessional even though it hadn't been painted yet. The little doors were hinged, the molding attached. The balusters spanned the width of the top.

"What do you think?"

"It's beautiful," I replied, and I looked at his dry hands, so artful and soft.

"Want to try it out?" he asked playfully. And he opened the narrow door. I stepped inside. I heard Wallace open the other door and then we were separated only by the foggy screen.

"Go ahead." He laughed.

"What am I supposed to say?"

"Say 'Forgive me, Father, for I have sinned.' "

"Forgive me, Father"—I giggled—"for I have sinned."

We were silent for a moment, and suddenly a heaviness washed over me. I wished to myself that Wallace could *be* my father, but more than that, I wished that he would come into my side of the confessional and stroke my head.

"I'm waiting," he called after a moment, but it seemed the cheer had left his voice, and I felt cold.

"Waiting for what?"

"For you to tell me your sins." His voice was serene. Suddenly, I felt flooded with an ache, and I wanted to tell him the things I'd done wrong. I dug my fingernails into my forearm to clear my head.

"Wallace," I called. "Wallace, I can't do this."

"Can't do what?"

"I can't do this," I choked.

"It's okay," he said. "You don't have to say anything. Why don't you be the priest? Is that okay?"

"Uh-huh."

Then he cleared his throat and said quietly, "Forgive me, Father, for I have sinned." And his words rolled out like the fronds of young ferns, so exposed.

"I forgive you," I called back through the cloudy window. I could hear him breathing heavy, and I closed my eyes and imagined myself holding him on my hip like a baby and feeling his breath tickle my ear.

"I'm having desires in a sacred place," he whispered.

"Sometimes desires are sacred thoughts," I told him.

We sat without speaking, and I continued to hear the

air pass in and out of his nose until it didn't sound like breathing at all. It sounded like something else.

"It's my turn," I called. "Forgive me, Father, for I have sinned."

I waited for him to respond to me, and when he didn't, I thought perhaps he wasn't there anymore. I worried that he'd never been there and thought I might have made him up. I thought I might be trapped inside a tree.

"Wallace, did you hear me? I said '*Forgive* me, Father, for I have sinned.' I wanted . . . I think I want—" and my voice broke. I slumped into my side of the confessional. My lungs felt full, but my legs felt fuller. I heard Wallace rise and open the door.

He entered my side of the confessional and pulled the door behind him. "Could I just hold you?" he asked, and I buried my head in his chest.

No air for me, no air, no room to cough, eyesblur-fuzz out. Wet. Corners pulling, tearing, widen my frown.

Who knocks? Who knocks against my throat? Throat-basher. Mouth full of bigbadwolfpaw. Mouth full of throat—basher—throat—basher.

Tug my hair like weeds. Hands squeeze my head. Push me down to my toes where there's no room.

Bad sounds. Mine and his. Chokes and gags all mine. Moans all his.

"Jael, are you okay?" Wallace asked, but I didn't lift my head. My face was buried in the soft flannel of his chest, and I nuzzled my nose into the space between buttons where the material overlapped. I nodded.

"What's the matter? What's wrong?"

I could feel my nose running and Wallace's shirt absorbing the dampness. His arms braced my back, and he pulled me closer to him.

"Just don't let go," I said.

"Did I scare you when I closed the door?"

I gestured no.

So we stood there inside the little room, and Wallace rubbed his chin across the top of my head. And he held on.

I rested on the cold floor of my stone room, my eye telescoping through the hole I'd chipped larger. I'd been watching the women for weeks, their shoes walking slow to their places, their dress shoes, their tennis shoes, their boots. Sometimes, they pulled their shoes off and sat in their pain sock-footed. Sometimes their hands caressed their feet while they listened quietly to someone else's wisdom.

I could have seen a face, from time to time, if I'd tried. But I never looked.

On that night, after they had read their rules, repeated their definitions, and said their opening prayer, after the moment of silence and after a woman had said, "Hi, I'm Jill," and the group had welcomed her with their predictable "Hi, Jill," and after the woman had begun to speak, the door squeaked open loudly, marking a latecomer's arrival.

Jill hushed.

The great brown loafers tapped across the floor, stopped, and settled between the legs of a chair. No one spoke, and I drew in my breath fearfully at the size of those shoes. I imagined what large and hairy feet hid inside. I imagined the hard yellow toenails.

Though I did not know what Jill looked like, I could imagine the panic on her face. I could feel her panic rush through that room and slap me as it whooshed between the stones and contaminated my own air.

After an uncomfortable minute, she stammered, "I just think that maybe—" and then, "I pass."

The woman sitting on the floor at Jill's feet took her foot and began massaging it, slowly, methodically. No one spoke.

I'd never known a man to attend the meetings before. Even in my safe space, I cringed.

The too-large loafers fidgeted. I wanted to yell out to him, to tell him to leave. But it wasn't his fault that his feet grew long and wide. I could see his fear reflecting off the shiny leather.

At last, the meeting continued.

"Hi, my name is Margaret," someone said.

And the shaky voices echoed, "Hi, Margaret."

I whispered to myself, "Hi, Margaret."

"My family's coming to visit this weekend, and I'm really scared because they've never been to my house before—not since I moved here—and I'm worried that something will go wrong. They won't like my furniture, or they'll hate the foods in my refrigerator."

As I listened to her talk, I could hear in her voice an anxiety that had nothing to do with her family's visit. She was speaking out of obligation. She was simply the volunteer, the sacrifice.

"I thought it wouldn't bother me—for them to come here. My abuser, my stepfather, died last year. But I realize that I don't want to see my *mother*. I'm so mad at her—still."

And as the meeting went on, the emptiness of their words resounded again and again. Different women spoke, but the trust that usually enabled them to scream or cry, the passion within their words, was gone. Though they all said different things, I couldn't tell them apart.

Finally, just a few minutes before the meeting ended, the man spoke up.

"Hi, I'm Joe, and I'm an incest survivor," he said.

A chorus of quiet "Hi, Joe" dissipated throughout the room.

"Hi, Joe," I echoed in my head.

"I didn't realize that this was a woman-only meeting, and I want to apologize—for surprising you. And for coming in late."

He paused, and it seemed I could hear a collective shiver.

"It's hard to find this kind of support when you're a man. Hard to know where to go. Hell, it's hard to be in this room right now, knowing you're all scared of me and knowing that I'm just like you in so many ways."

He crossed his feet.

"So I just wanted to say that. If any of you know

about a group for men or for men *and* women, I'd appreciate it if you'd let me know. I pass."

When the meeting ended, I watched red pumps and blue high-top tennis shoes approach the large leather shoes. They talked to him then. They were relieved that he was not some sick misogynist getting his kicks. Maybe they even knew of a group for him.

But Jill hurried away, her feet moving briskly outside my view. And I wished that I could invite her in for hot tea, offer her a chunk of wood and a knife, tell her to chop him up, to carve the madness out. But I was just another intruder, another who had heard the subtle crack of her voice.

I wanted to bury my head beneath my pillow when I heard her loud proclamation: "Hey, I'm Magdelena. I'm an incest survivor."

"Hi, Magdelena," I mumbled.

But there was no one else around. It was just me and the coffee-skinned woman sitting inside the tree. And I could hardly stay awake.

"I been having *ideas*," she slurred. "Not *real* ones. Made-*up* ones. I see a man in the laundry—hiding behind the washing machine. I slam his dick in the dryer. I slam it hard," she chuckled. "I *slam* it."

No, no, I thought, and I closed my eyes. I wanted to drop off into sleep, but my head kept spinning. I buried my head in my knees.

"Hi. My name's Mariah, and I'm an incest survivor."

You can't do that, I thought. You can't interrupt until Magdelena passes. But when I opened my eyes, the only woman there had a long braid and a broad backside. She sat in Magdelena's spot, but Magdelena was gone.

"Hi, Mariah," I replied groggily.

"Hello," she said again and smiled. "Today I've been having castration fantasies. I keep visualizing a man—hiding behind a tree. And I know he shouldn't be there. So in my fantasy, I grab his penis. I just grab it and pull him away to a pencil sharpener. And then I sharpen his penis like a pencil, and I draw him a picture with his own penis. It's a picture of my soul. The lines are so beautiful, but it's all bloody. And I make him look at it. And I say to him, 'Look at this. Look at what you've done.' "

I thought to myself, Don't listen. I thought, Go to sleep. And I said aloud—even though I'd learned the rule of not interrupting when someone else was speaking —I said, I cannot listen.

"Hi, I'm Mary."

"Goodnight, Mary."

"Hi, I'm Mary," she persisted. And I saw the Virgin there, her robe as red as—

". . . an incest survivor," she said.

Wallace had drawn me a map to his house. I had to walk to the street in front of the church, take a left, walk three blocks, take a right, and walk two more blocks. He'd told me to leave half an hour before dark, but I was late. By the time I approached his house, I could see the hazy sun glaring off the windows. The coldness huddled around me, and I wrapped my sweater tighter.

His white house sat in the middle of a block, with houses on either side and houses across the street. The steep concrete steps were too tall for my legs and reminded me of climbing up rocks.

I rang the bell.

"Get yourself in here," he said when he opened the door, grabbing my hand and pulling me inside the warm house. "Let me help you out of that sweater."

A small cat wearing a bandana around its gray neck pushed its way between my legs, purring, and walking around one leg and then the other.

"That's Artemis," Wallace said. "She's the baby."

I reached down to stroke her.

"I was worried about you. Thought you might have gotten lost. I was about to come looking for you in the car."

"Well, I'm here now," I said, not knowing what to do with my expression.

"Let me show you around, then."

Wallace led me into the sparsely furnished living room.

"We have here—the couch, the chair, and the ceiling fan." He swung his arms up towards the ceiling to direct my gaze. "And of course, we have my ceiling toys."

I saw the little jets and airplanes made of rubber or hard plastic dangling from the ceiling with pieces of string.

"What are they for?" I asked him.

"Just fun."

Next, he showed me the dining room. There was a shiny wooden table with four chairs and a fireplace, lit and crackling. The walls were decorated with art in different sizes and colors.

"Where'd you get the drawings?" I asked.

"The paintings? I did them."

"You're an artist?"

"Some days," he said, and he laughed. "I work construction to pay the bills. Art's a gamble."

I walked around the room to look at the pieces on the walls. I didn't think his art was particularly good. I couldn't tell if the biggest one featured a dog or a dinosaur. But one print I really liked. It was dark, like midnight, with a not quite full moon hanging over a wooded area where little purple figures danced behind great dark trees. I stared at it for a long time.

"You like that one?"

"I like them all," I said quietly.

"But you like that one more?" he asked, and I nodded. He seemed pleased by my choice.

"Come take a look at the kitchen."

"Smells good in here."

"Duck," he said, and I did, expecting a toy airplane to come zooming at my head from across the room.

Wallace laughed. "I meant dinner."

"Huh?"

"We're having duck for dinner."

The kitchen was large and open. Aside from the appliances, there was a full-length sofa covered with a blanket and a smaller table with two chairs.

"I like to cook," he said. "I spend a lot of time in here. You cook much?"

"I used to. But my apartment is so little that I don't fix big meals anymore."

"What's your favorite dish?" he asked.

"Huh?"

"Your favorite recipe—what is it?"

No one had ever asked me that before. I'd never thought about what I *liked* to cook. For a moment, it made me lonely, somehow, and nervous. I tried to think of the things I knew how to prepare. Fish. Eggs. Corn dodgers. "Pound cake," I told him, and he laughed.

Wallace did everything he could to make me feel comfortable, but he didn't realize that I wasn't accustomed to visiting in other people's spaces. When he invited me upstairs to see the bedroom, my air caught inside my throat for an instant. All the way up the steps, I repeated in my head the little prayer that the women used to open and close their meetings.

"What do you think of *this*?" he asked as he turned on the light switch. Against the far wall was the largest bed I'd ever seen. It was big enough to hold five people. And in the middle of the white comforter, Artemis was curled up next to a tremendous black cat, licking the fur on his neck.

"That's MacBeth," Wallace said. "I've had him for eight years."

"He's so big."

"He eats dog food," Wallace laughed. "When I took him to the vet—oh, I guess it's been eight or nine months ago—he weighed twenty pounds."

"If I were Artemis, I think I'd be scared of him."

"Oh, he *loves* Artemis. She's his baby, too."

We were still standing in the doorway, and Wallace stretched out his arm and motioned me inside.

I walked up to the bed, reached over, and rubbed MacBeth's shiny coat. He licked my hand with a rough tongue.

"They're good company. You have any pets?"

"I've never had a pet in my life," I told him. "Actually, I had a little turtle once. I kept him in a Lance cracker jar. His name was Sammy George Pickens—who knows how I came up with that one? When he died, I wrapped him in a dishrag, put him in a Mason jar, and threw him in the river. It took a long time for him to float out of my sight. The whole time his jar bobbed downstream, I sang church hymns. I think his funeral was the most fun we ever had together."

"You lived near a river before you came here?"

But I didn't answer him. Instead, I walked over to the head of the bed and ran my hand along the headboard. It was an intricate cast-iron grillework, swerving high and peaking at the center. It looked like something from a gothic castle. "Whoa," I said.

"You like it?" he asked.

"Where'd you get it?"

"I pieced it together."

I fingered the sharp and pointed corner pieces that looked like giant drill bits.

"I picked those up at a junkyard. Figured I'd find something to do with them. The piece in the center used to be somebody's gate, most likely. I just like to fiddle with odds and ends."

"It's kind of intimidating," I said, and Wallace

walked over, rested his hand on my back, and smiled his wise-eyed smile.

"It's just a hobby, Jael. Just a lot of junk. Did you see the ceiling?"

I looked up, and there were snowflakes dangling from silver strings. They looked as though they'd been cut out of paper, and I laughed at the thought of Wallace sitting at his table designing snowflakes. It seemed impossible that the same man could have designed the iron headboard and folded those sheets of thin white paper, bending the tiniest corners and clipping delicate diamonds without tearing. Only Wallace.

"There's more to see," he confessed proudly, heading out the doorway. I followed him down the hall.

"Here's the bathroom."

Even in its sparseness, Wallace's bathroom seemed to possess some sort of innate glamour. The walls were dull black and the porcelain tub and toilet were very old, clawfooted. There was a towel left on the floor, and it looked like it'd been dropped there on purpose. I had a feeling that all Wallace's mistakes looked that way.

"And here's the junk room."

He opened and closed the door very quickly, laughing. I caught sight of an ironing board and various boxes and some old broken chairs.

"You don't really need to look in there," he said. "It's a mess."

There were two other doors upstairs. The first one opened into a small room with only a daybed for furnishings. But there were three easels, each holding a painting in progress. Each painting featured a fish, but the fish were all different. One was a fish skeleton against a black background. Another was a multicolored fish overglazed in gold. The third was a fish-woman—almost a mermaid, but less fantastic.

"Where are her gills?" I asked.

"Right there," he answered, pointing.

"If I were you, I'd give her bigger gills, I think."

"Is that so?" He examined the picture for a minute, so I stared at it too. "You know, I think you're right. Any more advice?"

I walked over to the wall where several large canvases stretching across wooden frames leaned. "You *might* make her darker, I guess."

"You mean her skin?"

"Her scales."

"You do much painting?" he asked.

"Only in algae," I said seriously.

Wallace laughed and said, "You're a crazy one." I knew it was a compliment. I could tell by the way he stood with his hands in the back pockets of his jeans, admiring me like I was something he'd been looking for all over town.

When dinner was over, he took me into the other upstairs room—the wood room, he called it. It was the largest room in the house.

And I could smell the truth in that room, the pieces of driftwood and lumber and tree stumps and even balusters. In one corner, different varieties of molding, some square-edged and some rounded, littered the floor.

There was even a large cypress knee. It made me feel at home.

On the hardwood floor, wood chips rested on each other, blanketed in sawdust.

Wallace had three different saws, and all sorts of chipping, chiseling tools.

There was a bench made of sturdy sticks, and stools made of tree trunks.

"Those are for when I'm working," Wallace said. "I can't do woodwork when I'm sitting in a plastic chair. When I'm *on* wood, I can think like wood."

I nodded.

"I thought you might want to make something."

"What would I make?" I asked him.

"You'd have to figure it out for yourself."

"You mean now?"

"Whenever. You can come over whenever you want and work up here. I can get you a key if you like. . . ."

I sat down on the wooden bench and breathed deeply. The walnut wood, the cedar, the fresh pine smells and the heavy aroma of stains permeated the room. From my seat, I could see the silhouettes of branches outside the window, still as death but alive all the while.

Wallace sat down at my feet, his back pressing against my legs, and I placed my hands tentatively on his shoulders. It was still and quiet and I felt in my stomach the delicate flapping wings of a moth.

"So talk to me," he said finally, cocking his head back so that I looked directly down on his thin lips.

And I wanted to tell him everything, to toss my soul right into his hands and let him take care of it for a while. I liked the weight of his lean.

"This house is so wonderful," I said. "So big and open."

"The house is nice," he agreed. "It's been a big project, restoring all the rooms and painting. I had to rip out the floor in the downstairs bathroom—it was so nearly rotten when I bought it."

We were quiet for a while and I could smell him, the musky sweetness. I ran my finger beneath his hair to the place where the hairs began.

"Have you ever been married?" I asked. I could feel him stiffen.

Wallace chuckled and said, "*That* came out of nowhere, didn't it?"

I blushed. "I just wondered—since you bought a house and everything."

"Yes, I've been married. But not since I moved here."

"Oh." I tried to imagine what sort of woman he would have wed. I wondered if he looked this way back then—his dark hair hanging long, curling beneath the collar of his shirt, his eyes so sparkly yet heavy from blinking.

"That was years ago, and it didn't last long. We got married because we thought we were supposed to. Thought we were in love, I guess. It just didn't work out."

"Sorry I asked," I said, and he reached for my ankles and gave them a squeeze.

"It's okay," he answered. "So tell me how you came to work in the church."

I didn't have the words, or perhaps words were the wrong medium. I liked Wallace, and I didn't want to lie to him.

"I was in an accident," I told him. "And when I came to, I didn't remember anybody or anything. So someone helped me get this job, and I started all over."

I could see his dry scalp along the line of his part. If I put my nose to his head, I wondered if I could snort the dead cells up. I wondered if they'd tingle in my nose.

"My God," he said, "Jael."

Outside, the night was so clear that even the darkness seemed transparent. A thousand stars had collected just beyond the window panes, glimmering between the veined pattern of tree limbs. I looked at them and wished.

"I don't know what to say," Wallace whispered. "I had no idea." He reached for my hand and pulled it over his shoulder and held it for a long time.

My head screamed to me, You lied, you lied, you liar. But I closed my eyes and blocked everything out but the stroke of his thumb against my knuckle.

When we kissed, I could still taste hints of red wine. His lips on my eyelids, his lips on my earlobe.

Then, "Hi. My name is River Bill. Hi. My name is River Bill. Hi. My name is River Bill."

"Wallace," I called out and pulled his mouth to mine. I kissed him until the voice went away.

"Let's go to the bedroom," he said finally.

"No," I begged.

"Why not?"

"No," I said again, pleading rather than forceful.

Wallace pulled me closer, said, "Only because it would be more comfortable. We can stop whenever you want. I promise."

"Not the bedroom," I said.

"Okay."

His arms wrapped around me like vines.

"Do you mind if I kiss you again?"

For an answer, I brushed my lips across his neck, meandering in the soft skin beneath his chin.

Later, on the cool floor, he unbuttoned my shirt, and he kissed my breasts, and he breathed right onto my heart. I vowed to myself that I would not listen to the screaming in my mind. I told myself to concentrate.

"God grant me the serenity," I recited in my head, "to accept the things I cannot change."

He ran his tongue in circles around my nipple.

"The courage to change the things I can."

His tongue inched down to my belly.

"And the wisdom to know the difference."

"Oh, God, Jael—" he whispered as he discovered the big healed scar across my middle. And he nibbled it gently, tracing the thick seam with his tongue. From the way his leathery hands caressed my back, I could tell his kisses were in some transcendent way apologetic. He was trying to tell me that he didn't mind that I'd been slashed and patched.

"Did you know," I whispered, "that skin could clump?"

"Like cookie dough," he muttered.

His lips tugged at my scar's toughened width, unaware that I couldn't feel him, unaware of the nerves I'd
lost, the millions.

Blisters heal. This I know. Blisters seal over and
shrink, leaving only a pink place between your ankle
bones, above your heel, to testify to what they once
were. Even the Band-Aid glue disappears after a few
showers, peels away when you rub it. And then you
forget about blisters altogether. You can't even remember when you last had one, or what puddle of pores it
sprang from.

I've always preferred calluses to blisters because calluses protect and numb where blisters only run. So
many times as a child, I pulled myself across vines, arm
by arm, until my palms burned beneath the rough wood.
Later, I'd find the calluses, small but tough as the pads
of kitten feet, skin coagulated and perfect for nibbling.
Sooner or later, I'd reach the spot where skin turns into
blood. In my private game, the object was to nip the skin
without drawing blood. I rarely won.

That next Wednesday evening, I sat near the wall,
watched the therapy group, and gnawed the skin off my
knuckles. The women had mastered the art of dissocia-
tion, of leaving their bodies on command. What I
couldn't figure out was why they wanted to forget it.

The women spoke in paragraphs, but I just had sen-
tences. I wanted to say that every time I was with Wallace, I could see the old ones kissing me. Every single

time. I wanted to tell them, but I was on the wrong side of the wall.

And I didn't know what language to use when speaking to hulls.

I ate my skin in tiny bites, bending my finger, then latching on to the flesh that wrapped over the joint. My tongue ran the horizontal rut as I wiggled the skin with my teeth to loosen it up.

The wrinkles on my knuckles reminded me of penis skin, and I hated it.

Around the room there were eleven of them. They formed an irregular circle. They had lost their sense of shapes.

They told each other hello again and again.

I was replacing the candles around the church one afternoon when Arthur came bouncing towards me. His stooped back and quick step made him look buglike and animated.

"Jael, my dear," he said, "how are you?"

"Fine," I answered. "How are you?"

"Very well. I got your note and thought that something must be wrong. What did you need to speak with me about?"

"Nothing's wrong. It's just that a friend of mine invited me on a weekend trip, and I was wondering if it'd be okay with you for me to take Friday afternoon and Saturday off. I'd be back by Sunday night."

Arthur scratched his chin and tugged once at his

collar. "I think that sounds like a wonderful idea. What city will you visit?"

"The coast," I told him. And I finished replacing the candles. "I don't think I've ever seen the ocean before."

"Yes, yes," he said, dreamy. "The ocean's beautiful —especially in winter. Everything's more beautiful in solitude."

"Well, thank you, Father. I think I can get everything done by Friday afternoon if I work really hard."

Arthur stood beside me awkwardly, gazing off. I wondered if he was remembering a time at the beach. I didn't know if I should say anything else, but I didn't want to walk away and leave him there.

I was staring at his collar, wondering how anyone could tolerate a binding about the neck, when Arthur asked me who I'd be vacationing with.

"Wallace Mulhern, the carpenter who designed the new confessionals."

"With *Wallace*, Jael?"

"Yes, Father."

"I see."

It hadn't occurred to me that traveling with Wallace would be a problem for Arthur. And I surely couldn't have lied outright to a priest—not in the church or anywhere else. But from his expression, I could tell he wasn't pleased. And Arthur had become a man I didn't want to disappoint. Although he made me edgy sometimes, I knew that he was good. I cherished his praises like gifts.

"Well," he said finally, "I hope you have an excellent time." And he patted me on the shoulder. "Don't forget to clean the choir loft before you go. Luckily, they're practicing on Thursday this week instead of Saturday. Those choir members act like such Protestants sometimes, leaving their garbage all over the place." He winked.

"Yes, Father," I replied, and he turned away. As he walked behind the main altar, I noticed that his shoulders seemed more stooped than before.

I continued about my work. Though most people couldn't tell one candle from another, I'd become adept at spotting scratches and dents in the white wax. I always examined each candle carefully and saved the smoothest ones for the shrine of Mary. As I headed towards her altar with the box of candles, I gnawed away the skin on the inside of my lip.

As usual, the Blessed Virgin Mary looked down on me with the sweetest benevolence.

"Hi, Mother Mary," I said. "I'm back to replace the candles in your altar." I scraped away remnants of other candles from the glass containers and dumped the shredded wax into a plastic bag I kept for myself. I couldn't throw the wax away. I knew that anything left long enough in the presence of the Virgin became holy. And I collected holiness.

"You wouldn't have to work so hard if the parishioners would stop dying like flies. More people light candles for funerals than at any other time."

I looked up at Mary to see that, once again, her lips had come to life, full and pink where the stone had been. She'd taken to talking with me from time to time, and her voice cut the air like a bell.

"Really?" I replied. "Who was the memorial service for yesterday?"

"A man named Vernon Osgood," she said. "Arthur did an excellent job with his eulogy."

I returned the candles to their places and began straightening the flower arrangement at Mary's feet.

"I think Arthur's upset with me," I told her.

"There's a part of Arthur that'd have you never leave the sanctuary, Jael. You'd spend all your hours praying the prayers that someone else wrote. He's protective of you because he cares about you. But you're in no way obligated to live your life for him."

"I'm going away with Wallace, Mother. Is that a sin?"

"Only if it *feels* that way. Jael, look at me when I'm speaking to you."

So I turned my face to hers.

"The only reason Arthur doesn't want you to travel with Wallace is because Arthur is afraid of love-making."

I drew in my breath. Mary's face was gentle, but her words were matter-of-fact.

"Don't look away," she demanded, so I returned her gaze. I saw her smile at my blush. "Arthur means well. He's a good man. But he doesn't know much about physical love-making. It makes him nervous. What the Church forgets to teach you is that you can't minister to the spirit alone. Don't neglect the body, Jael. Minister to the body as well."

"Yes, Mother," I said, and I stood back up. I didn't know how to respond to her. I didn't know why she was telling me such things. "I'll bring you a seashell."

"You'll *what*?" said Arthur, who was standing a few yards behind me.

"It was just a little prayer," I told him. "You scared me."

"Sorry I interrupted you." Arthur looked humored. "You have a phone call in the office."

"I do?"

I turned back to the Virgin, and she gave me a re-assuring wink.

"Who is it?" I asked.

"Helen Marston," he said.

We walked side by side out of the sanctuary around to the office. I kept peeking back because I could see the Virgin's aura following me down the hall. But Arthur never noticed, and soon it disappeared. Just before we parted, Arthur looked at me, his old eyes twinkling, and said, "So you've started praying, have you?"

I was polishing the organ when I noticed an odd-looking figure kneeling before the Virgin. At first, I paid the woman little attention. She was shabbily dressed, but I did not recognize her until she lifted her head and I saw the bloody place.

It made me angry for Mammie to enter the Ma-donna's white space.

I walked quietly to the Virgin's shrine, and I could hear something that sounded like women laughing from very far away.

There was holy water at the entrance to the shrine, and I submerged both hands and splashed it on Mam-mie. She dissolved instantly.

"She was evil," I explained to the Madonna.

"No," she replied. "There's no such thing."

"She hurt me," I whispered. "She didn't keep me safe."

"But she taught you to recognize safe places. She taught you to see the powers around you."

"And I hurt her," I confessed.

"There's definitely too much hurt around here," she admitted. "But things aren't bad or good, Jael. They just *are*."

Helen had said to call if I needed her. There were no telephones where we stayed. I didn't need her anyway. We set up our tent beneath a cluster of pin oaks.

Wallace had loaned me thermal underwear, and I wore it beneath my skirt and sweater.

We walked down to the ocean, and our noses ran salty, and the beach was swallowed by the pounding waves. At night, the waves turned black. We heard the waves clapping against the beach. Wallace said they were clapping for us.

I only panicked once—when we were walking in the foam at the very edge of the sea. I looked at Wallace, and for just a moment in the shadow-light, he had River Bill's mouth.

Then I saw a glimmering figure skirting over the waves. It reminded me of the Virgin, of safety, and when I glanced at Wallace again, he was no one but himself.

The wind swirled the sand in a frenzy.

Inside the tent, I could hear the wind rattling the tarpaulin.

Wallace put foam padding underneath our sleeping bags. We slept huddled like chicks beneath a wing. His breath was my heater, and I stayed warm.

"You remember when you told me about your pet turtle named—what was it?—Sammy?"

"Sammy George Pickens," I said. "He went by all three names." The words came out of my mouth in cold, cloudy puffs. Everything about the morning was gray.

"Did you remember that *after* your accident, or are there certain things that you just never forgot?"

Wallace stirred the corned beef hash, flipping it over to reveal its crispy backside. I wanted to be near him, near the warmth of the food, but I was caught, again, in my lie.

I had forgotten that I shouldn't have known about the turtle. I watched Wallace for a moment, his sleep-heavy early-day face staring into the breakfast he prepared over a kerosene stove. He knelt beside the device, balanced on the balls of his feet and stirring.

"It's hard to explain," I told him, shivering. With every breath I could feel the cold slice into my lungs accusingly. "I remember the turtle, but I don't remember much else."

Wallace lifted the corned beef hash from the stove, covered the little pot with its lid, and set a tiny frying pan onto the orange and blue flames. He broke the first egg, then the second, looked up, and said, "Do you remember the house you lived in when you had Sammy George Pickens?"

"No," I said too quickly. My lungs refused the air around me. I focused on my breathing and tried to draw the air in through an open mouth. Though I was getting some air, I wasn't getting *enough* air. I thought perhaps it was because I was squatting, but when I tried to stand up, I couldn't.

"Wallace," I called.

Tell him you lied, I said to myself. Tell him you remember River Bill and the drunk men, Mammie's little head broken open and bloody; tell him you remember hiding in the closet from the drunk men and Mammie's little broken head. Tell him you remember the quiet noises River Bill made—whee-zes, whee-zes, whee-zes —waking up to find him standing over you, watching your chest, waking up to find Mammie hiding in your closet, whee-zing, whee-zing, waking up to find the drunk men, little zippers broken open, the taste of blood on your lip.

"Yeah?" he said, and he handed me a plate of corned beef hash and eggs.

"Can we make love now?" I looked down at the sandy earth beneath me and nibbled my lip. I could feel my legs trembling, shaking like storms.

"Do you want to eat first?"

"No." I panted because I couldn't catch my breath. We had not made love before.

"Oh," Wallace whispered, and he turned off the stove, leaving the eggs that were still cooking to sizzle runny. When I looked at him, his sleepy expression had been replaced by curiosity.

I stood up, grabbed his hand, and pulled him over to a tree where I sandwiched myself between the cool bark and Wallace's warm body. Though I kept on my skirt, I eventually peeled off my sweater and tossed it to the ground.

Each time he pushed into me, I could feel the tree scraping my back, scratching against my skin. It was exhilarating. It was like being made love to from both sides.

And all I could hear was breathing—mine, Wallace's, the wind's, Mammie's, River Bill's, the tree's, the breathing of spirits. And I could hear the sea.

And I wept, cried, sobs broken by breaths stuck crossways in my throat. And though Wallace held me tight, kissed the tears, my eyes, my soul plunged out through the bottoms of my feet, falling through the world's floor right into isolating blackness.

At low tide, we sat on the beach. Wallace whistled to himself and wove seaweed into my hair, sometimes pulling too hard.

I pushed sand away with my feet, digging to dampness and then cold water.

"I wish you'd sleep with me every night," Wallace said. "I sleep better when you're there."

I laughed at him.

"What's so funny about that? Don't you sleep better when I'm with you?"

"I guess," I said.

"You guess? You *guess*." And he tugged at my hair. "Why won't you spend the night at my house? Father Burke wouldn't have to know."

"I'm not worried about Arthur."

"Then why?"

"Because I hate your bed," I said, and I laughed.

"What's wrong with my bed?"

"It's spooky, and it sits too high off the ground."

"I built that bed myself," he told me.

"Well, I don't have to like *everything* that you make with your own hands, do I?" I stood up and pulled Wallace to his feet. "Come on."

We went walking down the beach, kicking through millions of broken shells and admiring the grayness of the water and the opaque winter sky.

"Do you mean to tell me that as long as you live, you're *never* going to get into my bed?"

"That's what I mean," I snickered.

"Just because you don't *like* it?"

"Because it's too big, Wallace. You could get lost in there. Look at this." I bent down and picked up a tiny brown stone with two symmetrical holes on one side and four symmetrical holes on the other. "I think it's a little skull."

Wallace examined it, stroked it, and passed it back to me.

"I know a game," I told him. "What you have to do is pick up shells—but only shells you could worship if you ever ran out of gods."

"Okay," Wallace said.

"There's one more rule," I told him. "When you pick up a shell, you have to dunk it in the ocean and then put it in your mouth and keep it there until you find another one."

So we ran about the beach, our mouths heavy with sandy sea shells and sea rocks and pieces of sea wood. And when we had enough—ten or twelve new gods each—we sat on a sand dune and displayed our prizes.

It was nearly sundown when we left the sandy stretch. Walking back with Wallace's arm around my shoulder, I noticed that our shadows had grown long and thin. I showed them to Wallace.

"I'm going to stomp on your head," I told him, and before he knew what was happening I ran up to the head on his shadow and stepped on it.

We chased each other's shadows down the beach, sometimes dodging the foot and sometimes stepping right through the shadows and never breaking bones or leaving bruises.

"Imagine that," I said to Wallace playfully, "I can kick and stomp and draw lines right into your shadow and never touch you at all."

"It's because you're carrying those gods in your pockets," he whispered.

When Wallace dropped me off, my muscles throbbed and I could hardly stay awake. But after a long bath and a bowl of soup, I couldn't sleep. I remembered the bag of wax shavings from the used candles. So I climbed from my bed, found the pale slivers, and warmed the holy wax in a saucepan until the pieces melted together and grew soft enough to be shaped.

I stirred in my gods.

On a whim, I scooped up a handful of ashes from my fireplace and added them to the waxy, rocky concoction. The mixture darkened. I added more, and it grew thick.

I molded a statue of a fat woman, and before she hardened, I stuck some Spanish moss that I'd taken from those sea trees to her head. The moss-hair hung down as far as her feet, straggly and gray as a question.

Fresh water breaks backward when it tumbles over rocks, as though it regrets being forced forward at a pace it didn't choose. Even the tiny waves of boat wakes wave good-bye until they are reduced to a ripple and then nothing. But with salt water, everything is different. With salt water, the whitecaps race towards the tumble. And when that water waves, it waves hello.

On my first day back at work, waves tumbled in my mind the whole time I cleaned. Back and forth with the dustcloth over the organ. Would Wallace love me if he knew how tainted I was? Back and forth with the vacuum running over the crimson carpet. Would he even want to see me again if he knew I'd been lying? Hello. Good-bye. All that waving, all that tumbling made me dizzy.

Because I was behind with my tasks, I could not chat with the Virgin for long. As soon as I saw her, I felt guilty for having left her, so spotless, abandoned, and still.

"Last night when I got home, I took all the seashells I'd collected and mixed them into some wax," I told her, running my white cloth gently between her toes. "I made a little dark statue of a woman."

I looked up to see if she'd become human again, but her eyes remained cool and hard.

"Then this morning, I remembered that I'd promised to bring one back for you." I dipped my cloth in holy water and dabbed at the hem of her robe. "So I went over to the statue and saw that her left breast was my favorite shell. Not a shell, really. I think it's a tiny skull. I picked it out with my fingernail and brought it to you. Where should I put it?"

I looked up at the Madonna, expecting her to answer, but she didn't. "Here. I'll put it right here behind your foot. Can you feel it? It's just behind your heel."

Her silence made me shy, and so I finished delicately sponging her without speaking. When I reached her face, the light caught the tinest wet residue left behind from her bath. It glimmered on her cheek. Without thinking, I kissed her there. I let my lips rest against her face and felt the stone soften and become warm.

That night in my stone room, I took down the crude little figure of the dark woman, sat her on the hearth, and ran my finger lightly over the crater in her chest where her breast was missing. She was ugly and fat and bumpy with gods. I stroked her like a pet.

"Do you know?" I asked her jokingly. "Do you know where your lost nipple is?" And I pulled a thick

strand of moss over her shoulder to cover the amputa-
tion.

"What are you hiding it for?" she snapped. "Too
ugly for you? Hmmm?" Instinctively I scooted away
from her. She did not have lips.

"Put it back," she commanded. "The hair. Put it
back where you found it." So I carefully reached over
and flicked the moss away, revealing the scarred place
on her chest.

"How many times have you ever fixed a lie by hiding
it?" she asked. "Ever?"

"What?"

"Think, think, think," she scolded.

"I was just playing with your hair," I said defensively.

"Stop lying to yourself, Jael. You were covering up
what you thought was a flaw. If there's one thing you've
got to learn, it's to appreciate the flaws. In flaws, you
find the truth."

"The truth?"

"Something you don't know much about yet. Take
off your shirt."

"What?"

"Take off your shirt," she repeated.

"I don't even know who you are," I said.

"It doesn't matter," she contended. "You made me.
Now take it off."

Nervously I pulled my arms out of each sleeve, lifted
my top over my head, and sat shivering in my bra. I
could see the little hairs on my arms standing up.

"Now take a look at that big, purple scar across your
middle. Go ahead."

I kept my arms crossed and assured her that I knew what it looked like.

"Don't be so difficult," she persisted. "I'm standing in front of *you* with one tit. Move your arms and look at your scar."

Obediently I peered down at the thick skin on my belly, and then I looked back up.

"Touch it," she said, and I felt myself choke on the air in my throat. "Go ahead."

And so I allowed the tips of my fingers to graze the raised skin. I had forgotten the texture of its unevenness.

"I did it," I told her.

"I know," she grumbled.

"I mean I put it there—the scar."

"I know," she said again. "You were honest back then—when you did that."

I couldn't figure out what she meant, and so I didn't say anything at all. We sat in silence for a moment before the dark woman piped back in.

"Don't get me wrong. I'm not saying that slicing yourself like a Thanksgiving goose is a good idea. But at least when you did it, you knew what you were feeling."

"What?"

"Think, think, think," she told me, screwing up her face until the impatience made her even uglier.

"Who are you?" I asked her.

"You can call me Magic."

"That's not a *name*," I told her. "I can't call you *that*."

"Whatever," she said. "It's who I am. You can play with my hair if you like."

Drifting in and out, in and out of sleep, I wondered what Wallace would think about the talking dark woman. He wouldn't believe she was holy, I thought. He wouldn't believe she could speak.

But she was a truth.

I knew that Wallace believed in me, but I was a lie, and I couldn't remember the place where the lie and the truth overlapped.

I couldn't remember what to call the place where the river ran into the sea, where the water was only a little salty but trees grew thin and the tide moved over the earth like a teasing tongue.

Wallace teased me, resting naked beside me. He stroked my bare stomach for hours and refused me more.

"Don't speak," he said. "Let's not talk anymore."

And we held each other, moving together, wordless but knowing the flavor of shoulders.

Afterwards I dreamed that Wallace found demons on his tongue, and he couldn't swallow them. He couldn't brush them away. They buried spike-toed boots in the roof of his mouth and pissed abscesses into his gums. When I tried to kiss them away, my lips scabbed.

I was sweeping the foyer, dragging the broom across the hardwood floor and laughing to myself at the little particles of dirt that escaped into the cracks when Arthur came in.

"Jael," he said. "Helen called and she's running late. She asked me to tell you that she'll be here around two."

"Okay," I replied, staring at his collar, that marvelous island of white centered in the circling pool of black.

"She wanted to take you to lunch, so I told her that you could leave early today."

"You sure?" I picked up the dustpan from the corner and placed it next to the low mound of grit I'd collected.

"Yes, go ahead—when she comes. If you haven't finished your sweeping by then, just leave it to the Lord." Arthur laughed at himself. "As the fundamentalists would say, 'Lay your burdens down at the Cross.' "

Sometimes it was hard to tell if Arthur was serious or kidding. It made me uncomfortable, not knowing his tone. Whenever he made a wisecrack, I shut up, not knowing how to respond. And the pauses in our conversations were so awkward. They reminded me of nights when I sat on the porch with River Bill, thinking that the blank spaces were probably okay but worried that they meant something else altogether.

"So you're really giving me the afternoon off?"

Arthur nodded. "I'll be bringing in the cleaning service next week to do the windows and ledges that you can't reach. It's ironic, but when they're gone, the sanctuary looks like it's in a bigger mess than before they came. You'll be busy when they're gone because they leave all that dust from the columns and the windows on the floor," he explained.

"Oh," I teased. "So you're giving me half a day off to make up for the overtime."

"Not even *God* gives you something for nothing," he responded. "But don't quote me on that." He patted my shoulder and said, "I'm off to the hospital to visit the afflicted."

"Okay," I said. "See you later." I captured the pile of dirt in the dustpan and headed for the trash.

We were sitting at the lunch counter at a nearby pharmacy when I discovered the real reason that Arthur had given me the afternoon off. All during lunch while I was laughing with Helen about my beach trip, telling her how we'd raced down the beach, how we'd eaten in restaurants because we couldn't make the kerosene stove work right, she'd kept glancing at her watch. After she'd finished her cheeseburger and fries, she dabbed at her mouth with the white napkin, rotated her stool so that it faced me, and told me she had something she needed to say.

"What is it?" I panicked, wishing she'd told me before I acted normal around her. And before I'd eaten.

"Arthur's worried about you, Jael. He's afraid about this whole relationship with Wallace—although he really *does* like Wallace," she reassured. "Uhm—I don't know how to tell you this . . ."

I was sure I was being sent away.

"He asked me to make an appointment for you with a gynecologist."

Gynecologist? I thought, and I instantly felt the mus-

cles in my neck contract and clench together. Breathe,
I told myself, breathe, you're not being fired, so breathe.

"When he first talked to me about it—and believe
me, it wasn't the highlight of my day either," she confided, "he told me he thought you should have a routine
check-up—just to make sure you were okay. And since
you can't remember your background, I thought it'd be
a good idea too. Do you know if you've ever had a pelvic
exam?"

"No," I whispered. I was grateful that the lunch
counter wasn't busy. Pelvic, pelvic, pelvic, I repeated in
my head. It was an ugly word.

"No you haven't, or no you don't remember?"

"I don't know," I snapped, but I hadn't.

"Well, actually, I *think* that Arthur wants you to have
the opportunity to get on birth control—if you want it.
He can't say that outright, of course, since the Church
doesn't endorse birth control. But I know that he be-
lieves in it."

I didn't care how liberal Arthur was. And I didn't
care how many good reasons there were for me to see a
gynecologist. I didn't want to. As Helen droned on and
on about the procedure, reassuring me again and again
that it was simple, painless, and brief, I imagined myself
curled up in a tiny ball and hiding in the gap in the dark
woman's chest. If only I could make myself a god, I
thought.

"There's no reason to be embarrassed," Helen continued, though she'd lowered her voice and now spoke
conspiratorially. "These doctors see women all day
long. I'll even go in with you if you want."

"No," I retorted.

"Okay," Helen said. "So anyway, your appointment's in an hour but we'll need to get there early to fill out the paperwork."

"It's today?"

"Uh-huh. But not for a whole hour, and it's just across the street at the medical plaza, so you've got plenty of time to finish your drink and ask me any questions."

I put my mouth to the straw and peered down into the cup at the pellets of ice floating in the brown liquid. I drew some up into the straw but let it fall back down again.

"What if I don't *want* to go?" I asked.

"Well, you certainly don't *have* to. I don't want you to feel like I'm making your choices for you. I just thought that this way would be easier. You wouldn't have to worry about it in advance."

"What makes you think I'd worry about it?"

"You don't have to go, Jael. It's your decision. I'll take you home right now if that's what you want."

Helen motioned to the woman behind the counter for the check. I poked at my last french fry, butting it deeper and deeper into the puddle of ketchup. Wallace and I had talked about birth control, but I was perfectly happy with the kind we'd used before, the kind that hadn't involved strangers sticking things in me. Freeze-dried, I thought. I felt freeze-dried, though I didn't exactly know what it meant.

"I don't mean to sway you one way or another," Helen said.

I forced myself to look at her.

"Arthur wants to make sure you have information—

just knowledge about how your body works—so you'll be physically safe—and emotionally. If you go to the doctor, I think he'll back off, spend less time worrying over you and Wallace."

"Oh," I said.

"Have you made up your mind?" she asked.

"Doesn't feel like it's mine to make up."

"Jael—"

I wasn't being fired, I reminded myself. I wasn't being sent away. Not yet.

I nodded and moved towards the door.

The waiting room was blue. I'd have felt better if it'd been brown. There was a small aquarium on the table to my left, and a single red fish swam around inside. Its fins and tail draped down like something menstrual.

When the woman called my name, Helen asked again if I was sure I didn't want her to go with me.

I was sure.

I stood on the scale. I peed in the cup. I followed the woman down a narrow corridor into a white room. She gave me a paper gown to wear and left.

The table didn't look long enough for a person.

I folded my skirt, sweater, and underclothes, placing them on a chair. I didn't get up on the table.

The doctor came in with a folder in her hands. She asked me questions about my medical history, and I claimed I couldn't remember. She asked if I'd ever been sexually assaulted, and I said no. She asked if I was certain, and I said yes.

She asked if I knew how my reproductive system worked. I told her I did, but she explained it anyway.

She asked if I had any questions or if there was anything else she should know. I wanted to tell her that when I made love, I thought I'd die, my chest all heavy. I wanted to tell her how faces changed—right before my eyes, how light turned Wallace into a stranger, a strangler. How he eased his way into my body and shoved me out through the top of my head.

I wanted her to know that I could flee.

But I didn't have any medical questions.

I didn't mind being examined. I simply did not want to be examined while lying on my back.

"Could you hop up on the table, please," the doctor said.

"Can't you do it with me standing up?" I asked.

She smiled and said, "That's impossible."

"Can you do it with me sitting in a chair?" I tried.

"It won't take long," she said. "Really."

"Can I just sit up on the edge of the table?"

She let me prop myself up on my elbows. I fitted my heels into the shiny metal rests, gritted my teeth, and became a leaf, falling deliberately and slow, riding the air like lint as she prodded my breasts and pressed hard on the outside of my stomach.

"Now I'm going to do the Pap smear," she told me from her rolling stool. "That means I take a sample of the tissue from your cervix and send it to the lab to make sure the cells are healthy. I'll just insert this speculum and swab the lining."

But when she slipped the cold instrument inside me,

I bolted upright, said, "*No*," jumped off the table as she rolled backwards, knocking the lamp with my hand. And the plastic piece fell out of me, clinking on the floor. We both looked down at the speculum, splayed across the linoleum like modified barbeque tongs.

"It was almost over," she claimed.

"No, it wasn't," I replied, and I grabbed my skirt and pulled it on underneath the paper gown.

"I screwed up," Helen said. "I should never have made the appointment without talking with you first." She kept running her hand over her forehead, pushing back the hair that was already pulled away from her face with a barette. "You have every right to be angry."

I was surprised. I had expected her to be mad with *me*.

"It'll probably make you feel better if you go ahead and release your anger. That's better than keeping it inside."

But I didn't exactly feel angry with Helen or with Arthur either. I felt numb, and when I tried to wiggle my toes inside my boots, it was like they didn't even exist.

"Please talk to me."

"I'm not mad, Helen," I said calmly.

"Of course you're mad. You have every *right* to be mad."

"I'm not *mad*," I shouted. "Not at you, anyway. I'm *mad* that she couldn't do the exam with me standing up. I'm *mad* at the people who make those stupid examining tables. I'm *mad* that she wouldn't let me stick the thing between my *own* legs. I would have let her look once I got it in," I sheepishly added.

We came to a red light, and Helen stopped the car.

"You want to go somewhere and talk?" she asked.

"How close are we to the river?"

"Not so close, and it's getting dark. But there's a lake near my house. Will that do?"

I nodded, and we drove there. All the way, I thought about what the dark woman had said about lying. Her words were leeches on my soul.

You're crazy, I told myself. You're completely crazy, talking to statues, to little wax figures. Hearing them talk back to you. It's punishment for the lies. Don't listen to what they say. If they aren't real, they can't possibly speak the truth.

Helen parked the car in a gravel driveway that ended at a footpath. We got out and walked down the path in semidarkness until we came to the lake. A few people strolled around its edges, walking dogs or just musing at the water's edge. Helen led me out on a dry grass peninsula, and we settled onto the cold earth. I rubbed my hand against the almost brittle winter blades. The words I needed to say to Helen thickened in my mouth.

"So what's the difference in being examined on a table and being examined standing up?" she asked.

"I'm not sure," I said, "but it feels different."

"I think you know."

"Know what?"

"I think you know a lot. About lots of things. I think you know things you aren't telling."

I couldn't clear my head. Everything about my life

seemed fuzzy—like it must be somebody else's life, or a dream. "Arthur's an asshole," I said, but not in an angry way.

"Why do you say that?"

"I don't know. He just is. I can't tell when he's joking or when he's being serious."

"He's usually joking," Helen said, "unless he's giving a sermon. And sometimes he jokes then, too. It's his way of dealing with the world."

"I didn't know priests could do that."

"Joke? I think Arthur thinks being a Catholic is funny."

"But he's a priest."

"So what?"

"He's supposed to be serious and spend his time instilling values in his congregation. Not sending me to a gynecologist."

Helen was suddenly very serious. "Jael, he didn't think of that as a joke. He surely didn't mean it to be hurtful. Just the opposite."

"I know. I'm being a jerk. I don't know why."

"I think I understand," Helen said. "But Arthur cares about you. He really does. And I think he wants the best for you."

I stood up, picked up some rocks, and began throwing them into the lake, one by one, listening to each one splash and then sink. I could tell I'd made her uncomfortable and knew I had to break the stillness, change the subject.

"I can hear them sinking," I told her. "Can you?"

"No," she said, and she listened as I tossed another one out. "What does it sound like?"

"Real faint. Like pinching your neck and exhaling."

I threw a few more rocks and sat back down.

"Do you think I'm crazy?" I asked her.

"For what?"

"Just generally crazy. Like for thinking rocks make noises on their way down. Do you think that's nutty?"

"I don't know," she replied.

"But you're *supposed* to know. You're a shrink."

"I'm a social worker. *Big* difference. Plus, I'm just getting started. So don't put too much pressure on me," she laughed.

"Do you think it's crazy to talk to things that aren't alive?"

"Maybe," Helen said.

"Because they can't hear, right? Like this rock. When I say, 'Good-bye, rock. Have a nice trip down,' it can't know what I mean, can it? It can't feel what I'm wishing, right? It can't talk back. So am I crazy?"

I skipped the rock four times when I threw it, and Helen was impressed. She stood up then, and we headed back up the path. Frogs cried from their homes within the reeds, and Helen panted as she trudged her weight uphill.

"Like the moon, Helen. Didn't you ever talk to the moon?"

She shook her head.

"So if I ask the moon questions and believe I hear answers, am I crazy?"

She stopped and looked skyward.

"You know," she said, "most people would probably call you crazy. But wise spirits take their chances."

That same night while I was sleeping, I dreamed that the dark woman called out to me.

"It hurts," she cried, her rough hands grabbing at the place where her breast should have been. "It hurts. Do something. Find something to fill it."

I couldn't find anything the right size. It had never hurt her before.

"Take this," I told her, thrusting one of my ovaries into her chest. It fit like a ball in its socket.

Then the pains hit me, deep in my abdomen, gnawing at the emptiness there, and I cried, "It hurts. God, it hurts."

So the dark woman gave me her right breast. It was an awkward fit, but the ache subsided.

Until her pain returned, and I had to give her my other ovary.

I woke up bleeding, and the cramps made my mouth water. I didn't fall asleep again but remained in that desperate place between waking and dreams, my knees pulled up to my chest. Behind my eyes, all I could see were speculums, waiting to open me up and milk me dry.

I told myself I wasn't like them. I promised myself that I wouldn't listen from behind the wall anymore. What kind of fool are you, I thought. Spending your time eavesdropping on a bunch of molested people. Still, I listened for their approaching noises.

My uterus knotted up as a piece of the bloody lining ripped away and made its painful journey downward. I understood the way my body worked—designed to make me nauseous and keep me doubled. No gynecologist needed to tell me about cycles. I kept records with the moon.

Sitting on the floor with my watercolors and sketchpad, I tried to paint a picture of my reproductive system. Ovaries to the sides, uterus pointing down like the skull of a heifer.

The women began to enter the next room, nervous like it was their first time though they came as regularly as menstruation.

"How have you been?" I heard.

Then "Okay. How are you?"

"Okay, I guess."

They were never fine. They never felt great either. Not on Wednesday nights. I pretended to be bored with their troubles as their meeting began.

Another pain hit me, and I went to the toilet, confused about whether or not I needed to shit. I caught the clot on a piece of toilet paper, thick and stringy like stewed tomatoes, but deeper red. I poked it with my finger, watched it shiver. I rolled it around the tissue and marveled at the amount of blood condensed in one jellychunk.

When I returned to my painting, I leaned against the wall so I could hear the incest monologues without necessarily watching, and continued about my work.

"Hi, I'm Lucy. I'm an incest survivor," the woman announced.

"Hi, Lucy," the group said in unison.

I wrote "Hi, Lucy" in pink across the top of my painting.

"I'm going back to school this semester. I dropped out eight years ago, so I'm a lot older than most of the other students, and I'm having a hell of a time getting back into the swing of things. One of the classes I'm taking, chemistry, it's really kicking my butt. I'm doomed in there. I'm failing that shit." She laughed. "But I think the whole situation is really getting to me. I mean, I go to school in the morning and have to work until eleven every night. I don't know, man. I don't know if I can do it."

There were no men in the room, of course.

She paused, and the group sat with her in silence. I washed out my brush and dipped it into the black.

"I know this doesn't sound like it has much to do with sexual abuse, and maybe it doesn't. But when I'm under stress—like school stress or work stress or any fucking kind of stress—I start having flashbacks like mad. I mean, I can be sitting in the middle of that chemistry class, doing everything I *can* to keep my mind on the subject, and all of a sudden—*boom*—I'm twelve years old and locked in my brother's room all over again."

The picture I was painting began to look less and less like a reproductive system. I'd started squiggling little lines here and there in black, and I'd given the ovaries horns.

No matter who spoke, I always felt it in my vagina. My vagina was the heaviest part of me.

"So the real problem I'm having—the one that's really scaring me, I mean—is that I'm having these urges, these *incredible* urges to hurt myself. I don't mean suicide or anything. I just keep wanting to burn myself with my iron. Sounds stupid, doesn't it?" she giggled. "But I *do*. Or cut myself with . . ."

I plugged up the hole in the wall with a cloth and turned on the radio.

"Turn that off," the dark woman said.

I ignored her, picked up my sketchpad, and turned it to a fresh page even though the other painting wasn't dry yet.

"I *told* you to turn it off," she demanded.

"Shhhhh," I scolded. "I don't want to." But I obeyed anyway.

"Heard something you didn't like, didn't you?"

"Could you lower your voice, please? They'll hear you," I whispered.

"No, they won't. Nobody hears me but you."

"I wish I'd never made you," I said.

"Shut up and listen to what they're saying," she told me.

The next speaker was Paula, and she claimed to have been raped that week. The silence of the other women hung thick with fear.

"I can't believe it, but I was *raped* by the utilities company. I got a bill this week for seven *hundred* dollars. I don't even have central heating. There is *no way* I used that much electricity. But try telling *them* that," she muttered.

"God, I'd like to slap her," I whispered to the dark woman. I imagined myself storming into that room and slapping her cheeks back and forth—because you don't tell a gathering of women who've felt their breathing halt as the fingers traced the elastic waistband of their panties that you've been raped by an electric bill.

"I can't handle it," she continued, her voice breaking. "I can't call them up or even write a letter because I'm feeling like such a victim now. It pushed me right back into my victim role. And I keep thinking—*why me?* Why am I *always* the one to be abused? I mean, it's been that way my whole life."

"Do you hear this?" I spit at the dark woman. "I hate molested people."

"Shhhhh," she whispered back. "Listen to what she has to say."

I wanted to run screaming into that meeting, to accuse her of making her own life miserable. I wanted to flip the sofa onto the coffee table that held the incest literature and break it. I wanted to scare her into her right mind. She was *not* raped. Not that week.

I could smell the blood coming out of me. I could taste metal in my mouth.

"I hate it when people try to trick me," I told the dark woman.

"Is that what she's doing?" the dark woman asked.

Instead of answering her, I plugged up the wall and began my painting again, this time using less water and more paint, so that the ovaries and uterus, still pink, appeared darker than before. I pressed my brush so hard against the solid circle of red that the bristles frayed.

"That's not dark enough," the dark woman said.

"It's as dark as I can get it," I replied. I was already annoyed, and the dark woman knew that she was provoking me.

"Why don't you use the real stuff?" she asked.

"What are you talking about?" I swirled my brush around in circles, gleaning as much red as I could. My knuckles were white with exasperation.

"Blood. Paint it with blood. Color-wise, you can't go wrong."

I looked at her, looked back at my picture, and continued with my watercoloring.

"You think it's disgusting, don't you? Because you aren't in touch with your body anymore. Anybody can paint, but you're the only one who can paint with your blood. Why do you think it's so disgusting?"

"I don't," I said, annoyed.

"Then go ahead," she laughed. "It's fun."

"You're crazy," I told her.

"You're uptight," she replied.

I threw down my paintbrush and glared at her, weird little fat wax thing, always insulting me. You're crazy, I thought. Crazy. But I was so irritated or maybe confused that I dabbed my paintbrush between my legs and swiped it tentatively across the page. The color was perfect.

"Try it with your fingers," the dark woman suggested.

So I did. And when a clot fell down, I spread it across the middle of the uterus like dough, stretching it and watching it thin at center.

"It's not dirty," the dark woman told me. "It's truth."

Besides the fact that my apartment was small, I'd never invited Wallace over for another reason. He was a man. And I didn't want men to enter my sacred space. But the longer we went out, the less tolerant Wallace became of the way I met him at the car when he came to pick me up and neglected to invite him inside when he brought me home. I told him that I didn't think men and women should be intimate inside church walls, but even that wasn't reason enough after a while.

And the longer we went out, the more confident I became that Wallace wouldn't desecrate my space anyway.

So I invited him over for dinner.

"My God," he said when he came inside. "It's just like you." And he wandered around looking at the different sticks propped up against the walls, at the feathers on the dresser and the squirrel's foot.

He made his way over to the fireplace and stared at the dark woman standing proudly on the mantel.

"You made this?" he asked.

"Yeah," I said, stirring the noodles and chicken I'd cooked together in my big pot.

"Such an odd little face and all that hair," he remarked, putting her down. "She doesn't have lips."

"So she won't keep me up all night talking," I said.

"Why just one boob?" he laughed, walking up and hugging me from behind.

"It's not a flaw," I told him.

We ate sitting in the middle of the floor, and when

we were done, I decided that I wanted Wallace to have my blood painting. As soon as the thought struck me, I felt light-headed.

"There's something I want to give you. A little present," I said. Then making my way to the bookshelf where my sketchpad was stuck between books, second thoughts flushed through me. I ran my finger across the cold spiral binding.

"Jael, where's your bed?" Wallace asked, looking around.

"In the bedroom," I answered, only half-listening.

"What bedroom?"

"In there." I pointed.

"I thought that was the closet," he said.

"It is."

"Let me see."

So I went over to the closet, grateful for the distraction, and I slid open the door and produced for Wallace my bed, neatly made and beckoning.

"You're a strange woman," he muttered. Then he walked over to me and sat down on the mattress. "I wish I could meet your parents. I want to know the people who made such a funny creature like you."

"*Creature*," I shrieked, and punched him playfully on the shoulder.

He grabbed me and pulled me down beside him. We lay back on the covers, and I tickled him for a while. Just when I thought he'd forgotten, he wiggled away and asked, "Hey, where's my present?"

"Huh?"

"You said you had a present for me."

"I changed my mind." I smiled. "I'll give it to you

some other day." I reached beneath his arm, pretended to count his ribs, hoping to make him laugh. But Wallace pulled away and sat up.

"No fair," he pouted. "You promised me a present," and he smiled, then puffed out his bottom lip.

"I didn't promise. I'll give it to you later." I tugged at his shirt. "Come here."

"Jael," he continued, "you have to give it to me. You got my hopes up."

"It's nothing," I said.

"It's something. It must be something." He rubbed his hand down the side of my face. Then he got excited again and bounced the bed up and down. "Please."

He was such a kid about it. It made me wish I'd bought him something impressive: a gas grill or a special screwdriver he'd always wanted. The longer he begged, the worse I felt.

The bookshelf was all the way across the room. The journey back to the bed felt like miles.

"Is it a picture?" he asked, his face glowing.

"No," I taunted. "It's a stuffed giraffe."

"Let me see." He grinned.

I felt like a first-grader giving the teacher a valentine. He took the sketchbook from my hand and said, "I guess my artistic nature must be rubbing off on you."

"Every chance it gets."

"Can I open it up?"

"No, wait," I told him, yanking the book away. It was turning into such a production. It wasn't happening the way I'd intended. "I need to explain first," I said, but then I didn't know what to say.

I opened the sketchbook and shoved it at Wallace.

"Huh," he said. Then "Hmmmmm." He held it up at an angle, then tilted it the other way so that the light from the room lit the page from behind. Cautiously, he ran his finger across the darkest marks, then turned the picture over to see it from the back. In several places, the stains had bled all the way through.

"What do you think?" I asked him nervously.

"What did you paint with?" he asked, intrigued, smiling, looking me straight in the eye.

"Not that I think I'm an artist or anything—" I said, looking down.

"You don't have to explain."

There was a long, tense pause. Wallace continued to stare at the paper, but I suspected he just looked at the painting to keep from having to look at me. I didn't know if he could identify the shapes, or if he thought he was supposed to. I needed something to put in my hands, so I grabbed one of his.

"Aren't you going to say *anything*?" I asked.

"What'd you paint it with?" he asked again.

"Coffee grounds," I lied.

"Coffee? Hmmmm . . ."

As he sat there examining it, I imagined the dark woman's disappointment with me. Not only a liar, but ashamed of my body, and not even honest with the person who loved me most.

"Not coffee," I admitted. "It's blood. From my period," I added quietly.

"Whoa," Wallace said. It was so silent in that room that I could hear the blood rushing through my arteries.

After a while, Wallace cleared his throat and found

his voice. "These lines—they're so rich—and so crude."

"Is that good?"

"Yeah," he encouraged.

I thought he might be holding off laughter, but I couldn't be certain. I wasn't sure what he thought was funny—that I had painted the picture or that I didn't understand his artsy jargon. I wasn't sure how to react. "It doesn't *sound* good," I said.

"It's perfect, Jael. It's exactly right."

"You think it's *cute,* don't you?" I asked. I was pissed.

"No, Hot-head. I think it's more than cute," and then he smiled in a pathetic way, like he didn't know what else to do with his face, and said, "No woman has ever given me her period before." And then he started laughing hard.

"You asshole," I yelled, and I reached to get the picture back.

He snatched it away, said, "You just don't get it, do you? I love it, Jael. I really do."

"Why do you act so amused then?"

"Because I'm a man," he said.

I wasn't sure about his tone.

"I wanted you to have it," I stammered. "But if you can't take it seriously . . ."

"I *am* taking it seriously. I *definitely* want it." He shook his head. "Such a strange creature."

I rested my head on his chest and played with one of his hands as he talked. His hand looked like an old map, with millions of lines and ridges. I wanted to nibble the tips right off his fingers. I thought that if I gnawed away his prints, no one else could claim him. I wasn't sure *I* wanted to claim him, but I didn't want anyone else to have the chance.

"I used to have a fantasy about painting with blood," he offered. "If I was a woman, I'd definitely do it."

I snuggled closer to him as he looked at the picture, then flipped to the page before where I'd tried to draw the reproductive system with watercolors.

" 'Hi, Lucy'?" he asked. "Who's Lucy?"

"I don't know," I claimed. "I was just being silly."

Wallace took my hand and began massaging the palm. I felt tremors.

"When did you start biting your nails?" he asked.

"Huh?"

"Your fingernails. They're all chewed off."

"I don't know," I said. "I think I've probably been doing it forever."

When Wallace put the sketchbook on the floor and closed the closet door, I heard the dark woman say, "Leave it cracked." I panicked for a moment, but Wallace just said, "Okay," as though the voice had been mine.

He was as gentle as ever, lip-dancing his way around me like I was some land that he had discovered and circumnavigated ten thousand times.

Then, Hi. My name is River Bill. Hi. My name is Zipper Bill. Hi. My name is . . .

The dark woman said, "Go in peace."

Arthur was right. On the day after the cleaning crew left, the sanctuary was a wreck. When I walked in and saw the dust shrouding the dark wood benches, I didn't even think to clean the statues. I spent the whole morning dusting the pews and vacuuming the cushions. Even the hymnals had to be wiped clean.

The holy water in the silver bowl at the back of the church was soiled. There was a special place behind the church where used holy water was supposed to be poured, but I poured it over my doorsteps instead.

I was on my way to the Virgin when I noticed that even the pictures on the wall had grown gray with the mist of fine dirt.

It was afternoon before I made it to Mary. She had collected her share of the particles blown down from the vaulted ceiling above her. Embarrassed to see her defiled, I quickly began brushing her off with my feather duster.

"Arthur means well," she said. "Do you know that?"

I jumped at her voice. I didn't expect her to speak with dust on her mouth.

"He really does. And don't act so embarrassed about the dust," she said. "Everything in existence is soiled every now and again. It's the price you pay for being here."

"For being where?"

"On the planet," she explained. "And what's so wrong with getting a little dirty once in a while?"

"*You* shouldn't get dirty," I remarked. "You even smell different."

"Different isn't necessarily bad. It's all a way of think-ing."

"I suppose," I said, unconvinced, and I moved down to her robe, gently swiping at her body.

"You don't need to feel so guilty, either."

"Guilty about what?"

"About ministering to the body," she said. "But don't forget to minister to the spirit. You can't choose one or the other. You have to find a balance."

After I left her, I went to the men and cleaned them as well. They were as cold and solid as death. When I passed over their flat chests, I couldn't help thinking about the Madonna's delicately curved one. And when I reached Jesus' lips, I almost forgot to wipe them.

Beneath the covers my ankles were crossed, and when I tried to pull them apart, I couldn't. I felt the throbbing in my ankles first, and then in the palms of my hands. I opened my eyes, and it was light, and I was in the woods behind the church, suspended from a cross. There were crosses on either side of me. The Blessed Virgin hung on one; the dark woman hung on the other.

Then voices became clear in the distance, men's voices, and I could hear the shuffle of many feet passing through the foliage, approaching.

Jesus was walking with River Bill, with Peter and Paul and Pius and Thompie Hayes. And the men from Mammie's store followed along with Arthur and Wallace.

Each man carried a speculum.

"We're safe," the Virgin called. "Our feet are nailed together."

"She's right," said the dark woman. "Our thighs are already closed."

"Shhhh," I whispered, "they'll hear us."

"They can't hear what we're saying," the Virgin cried back.

"They only hear with their ears," the dark woman added.

And when the men reached the crosses, they stood before us, deaf and stupid, looking at their instruments and each other, wondering what to do.

We were rattling down the street in Wallace's station wagon when he asked about my old boyfriends.

"I can't remember," I said.

"If you try really hard, can you recall feelings—or sensations—anything?"

"No," I answered, but I said it defensively. I had no patience for Wallace when he trespassed into my background. It was too hard to remember what I wasn't allowed to say. "For all I know I could have been a hooker."

"You're such a bitch sometimes."

"Do you think you could find a little empathy anywhere in your thick head?" I replied. "I may have *been* a hooker. I wasn't kidding."

Wallace turned the blinker on so hard I thought the

switch might pop off the steering column. I could always tell when he was really mad by the way he handled the car.

"You weren't a hooker, damn it."

"You can't know that," I retorted.

"Whoever you were, whatever you were, you still had the same body, the same mind, the same ways. You're the same *person*, without the memories. And you aren't the kind of *person* who would have been a hooker. So shut up about it."

"I *could* have been," I argued. "There are all kinds of hookers."

Wallace didn't turn down his street. Instead we drove through the neighborhood, quieting down, thinking, I guess.

Something he said hung around in my air. The part about being a person without memories. I had memories, of course. Plenty of them. But for the first time I realized that *that* was what I'd wanted when I arrived at the hospital. No memories. Nothing to remind me. That was why I'd faked amnesia in the first place. It alarmed me.

Wallace reached over, touched my thigh, and I didn't pull away. It was a nonverbal way of making up. He steered us back towards his house, parked the car, and we got out.

"Do you think you can ever be happy—without your memory, I mean?" I heard a mourning seep out of his voice, and an ache rose up from my abdomen into my chest.

"I'm happy now," I told him.

Wallace opened the back of the car, grabbed hold of one end of a pine log, and pulled it out.

"Can you catch that end?"

We walked up towards the front door, heaving the heavy wood that Wallace had cut for a project. He walked backwards, facing me, but I couldn't return his gaze. I focused my attention on his lower arms, those tight muscles flexed by the weight of the log. My hands burned.

"Are we taking it upstairs?" I asked.

"Do you think you can carry it that far?"

"Don't underestimate my strength," I said playfully, but Wallace didn't laugh.

We hurried up the stairs as quickly as we could, only stopping once for me to rest my arms. By the time we put the log down in Wallace's studio, we were both panting. I plopped down on the pine, and Wallace sat beside me.

"I'm sorry," he said. "I just keep hoping . . ."

"I know." My arms wouldn't stop shaking.

"It's cold," he said. "Did you close the door?"

"Didn't have a free hand," I told him.

I stayed in the studio while Wallace went out to the car to collect some other things. From the window I watched him crawl into the back of the car and rummage around, filling a paper bag with tools and cans of stain.

Liar, I thought. How can you lie to him when he's so open?

I watched him slam the car door and head back up the walkway, his face pure and his healing hands. Though

I was inside, I couldn't stop shaking. I couldn't get warm in spite of the guilt suffocating me hot.

When he returned to the room where I waited and saw me huddled crying on the floor, he said, "I'll be right back," and then I heard the water running.

Wallace led me to the bathroom, helped me out of my clothes, and held my arm as I stepped into the tub.

"Easy," he said.

"I'm sad," I blurted out.

"It's okay," he replied, and he dipped a cloth in the hot water, then squeezed it over my back. "I'm right here."

"I'm not dirty," I stammered.

"I know."

"These dreams," I said. "Sometimes I get them."

"Lie back," he told me, guiding my head into the water. "You just need to slow down."

"Sometimes you're in them," I cried. "With all the other men. You're just like them."

"In the dreams?" he asked.

"Sometimes," I said.

"Slow down," he coaxed.

Then in slow motion I saw his hand and the cloth come up towards my face, getting bigger and so close I could feel the warm of it.

Wet on my face, rag on my face, scrub my lips right off, no way to talk, no way to scream, wash my lips right off my dirty mouth.

Wormy-eyed old man, stubbled chin, cuts his shirt-

tail, wets it, scrubs my mouth. Water hose squirts, swish
and spit. Squeezes shirttail, wipes my lips off. Scrubs
mouth, eyes, mouth, rough and fast.

Wipes my words away. No lips to hold my words.

I sat upright, splashing Wallace with my movement,
my belly knotted with the fear.

"Hold on," he said. "Jael, what *is* it?"

"Not my face," I whispered.

"Okay," he tried. "I'm sorry."

I grabbed his hand, held it under the water.

"You're scaring me," he said. "You have to tell me
what's going on."

"I want you," I stammered.

"You *have* me," he replied, squeezing my hand
harder.

"No, I mean I *want* you. Now."

Wallace got up, moved over to the toilet, and sat
down. He looked at me and smiled, but his eyes held
something I'd never seen before. He looked lost, and he
looked like a child, and he was about to cry.

"No," he said. "I can't make love. Not when I don't
understand what's behind it."

His words were barbs in my skin. The bathroom
mirror steamed with his hurt. I had never known such
sadness before.

"We have to talk," he told me. "Will you talk?"

I buried my face into the crevice between my knees.

"Will you *talk* to me?" he demanded, and he was
crying. "Can you at least try?"

I stood up dripping, and he brought me a towel, cocooned it around me, and kissed me on the head.

Wallace knew how I disliked his gothic bedroom with the awful cast-iron headboard, so he remodeled his junk room for me. He put a straw mat on the floor, and a mattress with white covers. All around the room there were houseplants and potted trees, and the air smelled clean. The whole room teemed with life.

That's where Wallace took me when he led me away from the bathroom, and he tucked me into bed and rested on top of the covers beside me. And that's where I told him how I'd lied.

I told him how I lived with Mammie and helped her run the store until she died. I told him how a deacon from a local church had taken me in.

I told him how I'd lived with River Bill and how I'd run away.

"Why'd you leave?" he asked.

"Get under the covers," I begged.

So Wallace got under with me, and I turned my body away from him and backed up to him close.

"I didn't want to be his wife," I answered tenatively. "You understand?"

"Jael," he said, his voice quaking. And he sat up.

"Don't look at me," I warned him, and nudged him back down with my arm.

I told him about Thompie Hayes, and about how he'd left.

"Son of a bitch," Wallace groaned.

I told him about my home under the mother-tree, about living on my own and fishing and trapping and spying on the three women.

"Nobody believed they were real," I told him. "But I know they were."

"I love you," he said.

"Do you believe me, though?" I leaned my head back so I could see his expression. His eyes were full again, but the firmness of his touch told me it was for another reason. He moved his hand over the naked scar at my center. "Why'd you cut yourself up?" he asked.

"To pour the poison out," I said.

"What poison?"

"I don't know, exactly. That's just how I think of it."

"So you created the whole story—about losing your memory."

"I didn't want to go back," I explained.

"You don't have to go back," he reassured me.

"Will it be the same, now that you know?"

"No," he replied, throwing his leg over mine.

"Wallace," I said.

"It's okay," he told me.

"Promise," I begged.

So he did.

I needed to see their faces. I needed to know the shapes of their noses, the texture of their skin. So I stood on the back steps of the church with my broom in my hand, sweeping as the first of the women approached. I stood on the top step. I took my time.

The first one was nearing fifty, and she smiled at me with gapped teeth as she walked inside.

I moved down a step as three more women arrived, each one carrying a drink in one hand, a stuffed animal in the other. They spoke about someone's sick husband as they passed me, hardly noticing me at all.

I swept harder, sending the grit from their shoes out into the open air, thinking that they were stupid, pouty women, coming to the meeting to wallow.

Two more women walked up, but they lit cigarettes at the entrance and stood talking.

I was forced to sweep at normal speed.

I couldn't get over how typical they looked, their brown hair and golden hair. They could have been at church for choir practice. They could have been mothers waiting for their children to return from youth group. There was nothing separating them from any other woman I had ever met. Except they, too, carried stuffed animals.

I memorized their shoes.

One woman dropped her cigarette on the ground and stamped it out. The other woman followed, then noticed me, bent down, and picked up the butt.

There was no trash container by that entrance.

Awkwardly, I said, "I'll take those for you."

The women looked embarrassed as they placed the burned-out butts into my hand. I recognized the lines around their eyes. I recognized the angle of their slumps.

Instead of watching the meeting from inside my stone cell, I sat outside on the concrete steps where the women had entered the church. I knew how long it took to read the affirmations, the definitions, the rules. I knew when it was time for them to say their prayer. And though I couldn't hear them from outside, I held myself especially still during the opening silence.

A light wind picked up and it grew cooler. I could see the goose pimples erect on my arms, the tiny hairs stiff and paying respect to the onslaught of darkness. Above my head, the lightbulb hissed. I put my hands on the cold concrete, felt the sandy, holy place where their feet had passed.

I wondered what I would say to them—if I ever actually spoke. "Hi, my name is Jael, and I've been watching you for months." Or maybe, "Hi, my name is Jael, and I already know the things you dream." My body felt numb, and I hated myself for not having the nerve to walk into that room. In my mind, the door behind me stood as tall as a tower, and thick. My arms seemed weak.

Stupid women, I thought. Carrying around stuffed animals.

I had one of Wallace's sweatshirts tied around my waist, but instead of putting it on, I balled it up and held it in my lap. Above me, the thin slit of moon balanced on its curve in the dark sky, its sharp corners pointing upwards as if ready to impale a falling god.

I knew that if I went home, I'd watch them from the hole in the wall. And I couldn't do that anymore, knowing the bodies to match the feet. I regretted having seen them. I knew that I would sit on the steps until their meeting ended and they passed me again, aching but cleansed. And I would sit there silently as they paraded to their cars. They would hardly notice me at all.

One woman had ridden up on a bicycle and had chained it to the lamppost before she went inside. I looked over at the bike, at its handlebars and seat. I wanted to touch it, to extract some sort of energy, or just to bless it so that when she rode away, she'd be somehow connected to me. I imagined letting the air out of the tires so that she would have to stay.

Pathetic, I told myself. I had nothing to do with my hands.

Shielding my face with my knees, I began reciting, "Hi, my name is Jael, and I'm an incest survivor. Hi, my name is Jael, and sometimes I get too scared to move. Hi, my name is Jael, and I cut myself up for kicks. Hi, my name is Jael, and I've lied to everybody."

"They move the meeting outside?" a woman asked, and I jerked my head up, shocked by her gravelly voice. She was standing at the bottom of the steps.

"Huh?"

"Don't you think you ought to take those feelings to the meeting?" she said. She stood below me, her hand clutching the rail, skinny and spritely, with heavy eyelids, wild gray hair, and Winnie-the-Pooh in her arms.

"Uhm, I'm not going to the meeting," I whispered. My heart inched up into my throat, and I could hardly swallow.

"Okay," she said. "But you made it this far. You sure you don't want to come in with *me*?" She walked up towards the door, looking back.

"It's almost over," I told her.

"There's thirty minutes left," she replied. "If you get here late, you can still go in."

"Oh."

I watched her grab the sturdy brass handle, her thumb pressing down, and the door creaking as she cracked it open. She made it look so easy.

"You okay?" she asked.

I nodded.

"You want to be alone?"

I shrugged. Inside I was quaking. I was too close, and I was on the verge of splattering. My body began to tremble in response to her question. I buried my head in my knees again and mumbled, "Why would anyone want to do this to me?"

The door closed quietly. She sat down beside me on the steps and said, "It gets easier."

I'd been sitting on the concrete for so long that my whole backside tingled. The woman sat beside me without saying anything. From the corner of my eye, I caught glimpses of her thin face turned up to the sky. We watched the dark clouds together through the hints of fog just beginning to settle above the trees.

"The meeting will be over any minute now," she said. "I don't know if you want to be here when they come out."

I didn't respond.

"Sometimes after meetings, I like to grab a friend and drink coffee. Can I buy you a cup?"

I didn't know her, but her face was friendly. So I agreed.

"You don't have to talk if you don't want to," she said, turning the car onto the street. "Whatever you need."

She drove me to an all-night café only a few miles from the church. We sat in a booth towards the back, and she lit up a cigarette, offered me one, and tapped her pack on the table. "My name's Arlene," she said. "And I've been going to the meetings since they first started, oh, about four years ago, I guess. You ever been to a survivors' meeting before?"

I shook my head.

"I didn't think so."

The waiter brought our coffees, offering cream and spoons. When he was gone, Arlene joked, "Got to watch out for those little suckers. They'll sneak up on you and listen."

I laughed.

"There you go," she said. "You gotta loosen up. Shake that tension on out. Find something to laugh about. Makes everything a lot easier." She ripped open a package of sweetener, dumped it into her coffee, and added, "This conversation will go a lot smoother if you'll tell me your name."

I could see twinkles swimming in her eyes. "Jael," I said.

"Jael?" she repeated. "I never heard that one before. I'm Arlene."

"Nice to meet you," I said, even though she'd told me her name already.

"So what were you sitting on the church steps for? Did you lose your nerve?"

"I guess you could say that," I told her. I dipped my spoon into my coffee and then dabbed it onto the napkin, making wet little flowers as I spoke. "Really, I didn't intend to go at all this time. I wanted to look at the people first. To see what they looked like before I went in."

"Why does it matter?"

"I don't know," I told her. I stared at her hair, noticing the way the frizzy curls dangled at her shoulders. "I don't know."

"It's always hard—the first time. Then you get used to it. You meet some people, get their phone numbers, even start going to the movies together."

"Do you know all those people?"

"Most of them," she said. "Same old ones come about every week. Every now and then somebody new will show up."

"I don't know if I'd have anything to say," I confided.

"Oh, I'll bet you'd have plenty to say. You were saying a whole lot when I walked up on you tonight. You might not want to say it at first, but sooner or later, you'll find the words. They come to you after a while."

"I already know the opening prayer," I said. And then I lowered my head because I felt very young.

"Well, that's a start. I tell you what. You can go with me next week. I'll pick you up and then I can introduce you to the others, so you won't feel like such an outsider. How does that sound?"

"Okay," I said.

"Good. Let me give you my phone number, and if you need to talk during the week, you just call."

I couldn't believe that someone who didn't know me would give me her number so willingly, but there she was, writing her name and number on a napkin in a tall black handwriting that reminded me of River Bill's wife's signature.

I took it and said, "Thank you."

She said, "Call any time."

"Will you be the one who answers?"

"If I don't, just ask for me."

"Will it make your husband mad?" I asked and instantly felt foolish.

"No husband," she said. "Nobody's going to get mad with you. Just call."

"You don't even *know* me," I murmured.

"I probably know you better than you think," she replied.

When I walked up to his office, the door was open, and I could see Arthur sitting behind his big wooden desk, talking on the phone. I stood in the hallway, fidgeting. I had never bothered him in his office before.

"Come on in, Jael," Arthur called, his hand covering the receiver's mouthpiece.

I shuffled into the room and tentatively sat down as he continued his conversation.

On the edge of his desk there was a book of religious

drawings and paintings. I picked it up and half-heartedly thumbed through. I was staring at a picture of a simple plate bearing two loaves of bread when he hung up the telephone. Feeling awkward, I pretended to be immersed in the art.

"Do you like that picture? It's Saint Agatha."

I thought he must be confused. I thought perhaps he couldn't see the page from the other side of his desk. I nodded to Arthur, wondering if he was beginning to grow senile.

"Saint Agatha was a virgin martyr. She was tortured to death in a brothel when she was just a girl."

"Why?"

"She cherished her virginity above the wants of the consul," he explained. "What can I help you with?"

"I was wondering if you have a map I can borrow."

"What sort of map?"

"Just a map of the city and the places around it. One with names of streets if you've got it." I traced the loaves of bread with my finger as Arthur opened some drawers and rifled through the papers.

"I'm pretty sure I don't have one here. I've got maps at home. I could bring one in tomorrow."

"If you've got one," I said.

"Do you need directions somewhere?"

"Not really," I told him. "I want to know what's nearby. That's all. Street names and stuff. How far away we are from the mountains and the river . . ." My voice faded.

"You'll be hard-pressed to find mountains around here," he laughed. "But I'll bring one in for you."

"Thank you, Father."

"Sometime this week, you might want to do the laundry."

"Okay."

"I'll take the altar cloth to the cleaners, but you can do the choir robes and also the alb."

"The what?"

"The white one that I wear for the regular mass."

Arthur nodded down towards the book in my lap. "Those are her breasts, you know."

"What?" I asked, looking up.

"They cut them off," he explained. "Agatha preferred it to sacrificing her chastity."

"My God," I muttered and closed the volume, placing it back on his desk.

"Some of those early saints, they understood dedication. Now if we could just get the acolytes to do the same thing, we'd be in good shape. Did I tell you about the acolyte last Sunday who got tired and left church? Just left? It was kind of funny, actually."

"They cut off her breasts?" I said. "That's outrageous."

I decided to do the church laundry with my own laundry, and so after I had collected the choir robes, I ran down to my apartment and gathered together my clothes.

"Better take a trash bag in case it starts raining again," the dark woman warned.

"It's not raining anymore."

"Better take one just in case."

"You're so practical," I whined.

Sometimes the way she nagged at me made me annoyed. But I was more annoyed with myself for listening to a wax woman. I shoved a trash bag into the pocket of my skirt, loaded the soiled garments into the wire cart, and headed down the street.

The rain that had been coming down for days had completely ended, and the air was warm. As I pulled the cart down the street, I noticed that the sun had toasted the sidewalks and almost dried them. But bits of mud still splattered against the hamper. I'd need the trash bag to cover the clean clothes on the way home. Once again, the dark woman was right.

When I entered the Laundromat, a homeless man sat hunched-up in a corner on a stack of newspapers. He smelled like buttered popcorn, but I knew the odor really came from urine. I separated the clothes into the different washers and added detergent, thinking about the woman with the thick slur, about the time she had led me to the farthest corner where the water from the machines poured out, about how she had said, "Men pee-pee there." I felt nauseous and decided to wait for the clothes outside.

I settled onto the Laundromat stoop with a fruit juice and the book of maps that Arthur had loaned me. Though the stoop was covered by an awning, the concrete was still damp. I could feel the wetness slowly seeping through my skirt, but the thought of staying inside with the vague odor of pee appealed to me less. I flipped through the maps, looking for rivers.

When I heard footsteps coming near, I looked up

and made eye contact with a strange man by accident. I knew I shouldn't have looked at him. I tried to never look strangers in the eye, give them that invitation. Then I felt guilty for being suspicious of every strange man I met, so I smiled. The man nodded and kept walking.

I had located the river and was tracing the snaking line with my finger when the man turned around and said, "Your skirt's going to get wet if you sit there for long."

My skirt was wet already. "Yes," I said. "Thanks." I'd never seen the man before but guessed that he was thirty or more. He was wearing an old blue suit that hung off his bones like a flag on a day without wind. His hair was rumpled, and although winter had only recently made its retreat, his face was tanned red.

No, no, no, I whispered in my head, hoping to either hold off the panic or hold off the man.

"What's your name?" he asked anyway.

I felt a shiver course through my legs. "Jael," I said, and looked back down at the map. Quietly, internally, I cursed myself for telling him my real name. I didn't know why men could sometimes reduce me to infancy or some other lenient, helpless state. Why didn't I say my name was Candice? Or Barbara? Or why didn't I tell him to "get the fuck away from me" like people say in movies?

"Jael?" He laughed. "I been there before. You ever been to jail, Jael?"

"No," I said and pretended to keep reading. With my eyes down, I reminded myself that he seemed friendly, that he hadn't said anything that should scare me. Sweat trickled down between my breasts.

"Well, I'm Mike," he volunteered. "Good to meet you. You live around here?"

"Not too far from here," I whispered, avoiding specifics.

"You go to school?" he asked.

"No."

"Me neither. I dropped out of high school my senior year. People say I'm crazy, but I've known that all along. Just couldn't take anymore school."

I nodded and reminded myself to breathe. I told myself he was probably just a businessman on his way home from work. I tried to imagine what the dark woman would do.

He stepped up closer, looked down in my lap. "Hey, do you like to read maps?"

"Sometimes," I said and pressed my legs together.

"Me too. I'm an explorer."

"Oh," I said.

"I been all over this land. You ever been places, Jael?"

I hated the way he said my name. I wished I'd told him my name was Arlene. I wondered what Arlene would say to the man. I tried to hold myself down.

"Tell me where you been. I bet we been to the same places."

I tried to think about something safe, about the inside of my closet, my bed and the heavy doors and the firm stone walls. Breathe, I told myself. Keep yourself calm. But I was already lifting.

"You ever seen the desert? Only water you see in the desert is your own piss."

Cold on my butt, wet on my butt, damp like dew, don't wet my panties. Wet in my panties and Mammie'll whalp, whalp, whalp at my back. That man pees in my mouth and don't let him pee in my panties.

Catch my breath. Can't breathe when he pees. When my panties get wet. No air for me. Pee goes behind my eyes. Goes sloshing, sloshing when I walk.

Then I looked way down and through the glowing, I saw the top of Mike's head. He was still talking, sitting next to the scared woman with a wet skirt and a blank face.

"I tell you what! There's nothing like sleeping in the desert. One time I was sleeping and this armadillo stepped right on me. You ever had an armadillo step on you? Feels like—" Mike broke off and looked away. "Hey, Ed. Big Ed," he yelled, motioning to an old man with a long matted beard who was riding a three-wheeler bicycle down the street.

"Mike, my man," Ed replied, pulling his bike over to the curb.

Mike turned to the scared woman and said, "I'll be right back, Jail-lady."

The scared woman looked down at maps. I knew she felt dizzy, and I knew she felt lost. Go inside, I yelled down to her. And she tried, but nothing would move. Concentrate, I told her. Lift your feet. But it took too much energy for her to breathe. I wasn't sure that she could hear me from so far away. She was too hollow to know what to do.

The air felt so comfortable. I didn't want to help her. I wanted to stay high with the brilliant, blazing gleam. I could see everything from there.

Mike and Ed were talking just a few feet away, and their voices slowly became audible to me as I settled back into my skin.

There were several bags in the baskets on either side of Ed's bicycle, and objects stuck out of every bag—a vase, an old game, some clothes.

"You got anything in that bag I could give to my girlfriend?" Mike asked Ed.

You see, I told myself. He has a girlfriend. You were worried over nothing—stupid, paranoid, subhuman freak. You're not even *worth* threatening. Always thinking you're so important. He didn't even do anything except sit down beside you and talk. You can't even *talk* to a man without splattering all over the place.

But another part said, Get out. Get *out*.

I sat there listening to myself, immobile.

Ed gave Mike a long, broken strand of fake pearls. Mike knotted the ends together, thanked Ed, and walked towards me again.

"Here," he said. "I brought you a present."

I coughed, took the pearls, and wrapped them around my hand.

"Aren't you going to put them on?" he asked.

"I'll just wear them as a bracelet," I said weakly.

"No," Mike protested. "I bought you a necklace. The least you can do is put it on right."

Obediently, I pulled the strand over my head. It felt caustic to the skin around my neck.

Mike smiled, picked up my juice, and drank it. "Those pearls look real nice on you, lady."

"I have to go check my clothes now," I told him.

"Want me to help you?" he asked.

"No," I said. "I can get them by myself." Panic settled in my mouth, thick like cream.

"Let me fold your clothes," he crooned.

I closed my eyes and begged to whoever was listening, "Please make him stop."

And then the dark woman stepped up, walked towards Mike, and said, "Go away."

"Wait a minute, lady," he argued.

"Go *away*," she repeated. "Don't make me tell you again."

I gave Mike back his pearls and followed her tough little body through the Laundromat door.

"Thank you," I panted and sank down onto a chair. I was shaking and hadn't yet noticed that the dark woman was nowhere in sight.

"You're welcome," the old man said from his newspaper stack.

"I'm never doing laundry there again," I told the dark woman. "What if he followed me home? He might know where I live. I'll have to move."

She stared across the room like something made from wax. She didn't even look at me.

I tossed my underwear and socks into a drawer, then pulled out a hanger and returned my clothes to the closet. I told myself to calm down and did the dishes.

I thought about how he'd drunk my juice, then gagged and talked myself out of throwing up. I decided I'd better call Helen, but when I dialed her number, I got the answering machine.

"I hate those damned things," I yelled, hanging up. Then I turned to the dark woman, inanimate as the past. "Would you talk to me?" I demanded.

"Not until you lighten up," she said, without moving or becoming real in the least.

"I hate men. I hate them all—their stupid power games and their hard faces." I checked the locks on the door. "What if he sees me somewhere? I don't ever want to talk to him again."

I called Helen and hung up on her answering machine for the second time.

"A church this big should have a washing machine," I told the dark woman. "And a dryer too. It's crazy to have to take all this stuff to the Laundromat."

I looked down at what I was wearing. A skirt and sweater. He'd recognize me if he saw me again. I'd have to come up with a new look. I'd have to wear a black leather jacket and motorcycle boots to keep him from recognizing me. I'd have to change my lifestyle. I ran my hands through my hair.

My hair. I found the scissors, pulled out the trash can, and cut it off, ragged and blunt, halfway between my shoulders and ears. Instantly I felt safer.

"Are you happy?" the dark woman asked.

"I think so," I said.

"You took the easy way out."

"What do you mean?"

"The wimp approach. You're trying to hide again."

"You'd try to hide too if you'd had a day like mine."

"Maybe," she said.

"I'd been thinking of cutting my hair anyway," I told her. "I had a knot in the back."

"Excuses," she said.

"He scared me so bad."

"I know."

"He was awful. These men, they're everywhere I look. I can't get away from them. They're like pit bulls that have learned to climb trees." My nose was running, but I didn't feel like blowing it. I didn't feel like doing anything except crying.

"You need to stop trying to hide from the things you don't like. Stand up to the fear. Look it in the eye. You can decide when it's okay to talk to somebody, and when it isn't, you can leave."

"I can't just walk away."

"You've got feet, don't you? And legs and a mind of your own—"

"It's not that easy."

"It's *that* easy."

"I get so scared."

"You did it today. It took awhile, but you walked away from him. You'll get better at it with practice." The dark woman ran her hand through her mossy hair, and I noticed that her fingers looked a lot like mine.

I repeated the gesture, tugging at some longer pieces of my own hair and then pushing them behind my ear. "It's uneven," I said to the mirror.

"It looks fine," the dark woman replied. "It's got some character."

In the night, I couldn't sleep, and I couldn't wake up. Again and again the big red penis moved towards my mouth. I could feel the corners where my bottom and top lips joined stretching and slowly pulling away. Little tiny girl with a mouth from ear to ear. It punched at the back of my throat, trying to beat a path through my head.

"You don't have to stay there," the dark woman called from somewhere far away. "You can wake up."

My words were stuck beneath the big worm, and I couldn't answer.

Then I saw myself, my eyes wet and my eyelashes glistening with the hurt. One eyelash on each eye wiggled like it was alive separately from me. I took tweezers and pulled the wiggling ones out, and they were red worms moving on the table.

In the distance, I heard the dark woman say, "You can kill them," so I smashed them there and smeared their guts.

Then I felt something moving in my eye again and saw that there were more worms waving in front of my eyes like antennae.

"Wake up," the dark woman cried.

Again I yanked the worms away and beat them with my fists.

"You can wake up," she repeated.

But I didn't have time. As quickly as I could pull them out, new ones took their places. And the big red penis began again to move in and out of my mouth. I couldn't reach my eyes, and the worms wavered and crawled on my face.

"You can change them into something else."

"What?" I called back.

"Flowers," she said.

"I'm turning you into flowers," I told them.

The penis-worms recoiled, a bit.

"I'm turning you into flowers," I insisted.

"Hyacinths," the dark woman cried. "Make them hyacinths. Concentrate." The pulsing in my mouth slowed down and stopped altogether. Flowers, I thought. There are hyacinths blooming from my eyes. It seemed that the wiggling had ceased, but I didn't budge.

"You can pick them," the dark woman said. "They've bloomed."

I could see the white light coming for me, her smooth radiance, her arms spread wide. "I think I'll leave them," I said, sleepy. "What color?"

"Purple," she told me.

"Nice," I mumbled, and I could smell the sweetness circling my body as I floated out to meet the Madonna.

I stood at the big sink in the supply closet, hand-washing the little white napkins they used to wipe the rims of chalices each time the congregation drank wine. The water was soapy and boiling hot to get out the red stains. I wore gloves up to my elbows and scrubbed the stains with a brush until they faded to pink and disappeared.

I'd been working for what seemed an eternity when I noticed a slight banging noise and looked up to see Baby Jesus sitting on the box of Ivory Flakes, kicking his heels against the cardboard and grinning at me. I blinked and looked again. He hadn't gone away.

"You always look surprised to see me," he giggled.

"I guess I am," I said.

"This is my *house*," he replied. "I'm *supposed* to be here."

You're a lunatic, I told myself, and I peeked behind to be sure the supply room door was closed before I continued my conversation.

"So what's up?" I asked him.

"I came to watch the bubbles," he said.

"Huh?"

"I like the bubbles." He hopped down onto the rim of the sink, dabbed his little foot in the soapy suds, and kicked. Some of the soap splashed onto my lips. I blew bubbles back at Jesus.

"I can't visit you anymore after this," he said.

"Why not?" I asked.

"Ask *her*," he said.

"Your mother?"

"Uh-huh. She says you won't need me in the same way soon." He kicked again, sending suds all over my shirt.

I reached into the sink, took a big handful of bubbles, and showered them over his head.

"In another life," he said, "I'd like to be a bubble. Wouldn't you?"

"Yeah."

"On a windy day. So I could do flips in the air."

"That'd be fun," I agreed.

"It'd feel good," he said.

"Sometimes I go floating, but I don't feel like a bubble."

"It's hard to be light as a bubble," he replied in his charmed little way. "But if you practice a lot, it could happen."

In the evenings, I went over to Wallace's house and we worked together in his studio. He was getting ready for a craft show in another part of the state and was building chairs that sat low to the ground—the kind of chairs that women in other countries use while they make batiks. Earlier in the week, he'd given me a piece of wood to keep me occupied, and I'd decided to make a drum. So we worked together. While Wallace carved thin strips of wood away from the seat, I hollowed out the inside of my stump.

"So did you tell Helen yet?" he asked.

"I haven't seen her this week," I mumbled.

"I told you to call her, Jael. You need to *talk* about all this stuff with somebody qualified."

"I don't want to tell her," I whined, and I held up my wood. "Do you think it would work better if I burned the inside out?"

"Oh, no, you don't," Wallace said. "You're not changing the subject on me. You need to talk to a woman about this, and I'm not leaving you alone until you do."

"Why does it have to be a woman?"

"Why do you have to be so hard to get along with? You're just trying to pick a fight. It doesn't have to be a woman. I figured you'd rather talk with a woman. Go talk to Arthur if you want—or anybody else. I don't care."

"I talk to *you*. Doesn't that count?"

"I don't know how to help you. Haven't you figured that out yet? I don't have a clue about what you need to do to work through all this stuff. Did you go to that meeting?"

"I tried."

"What do you mean, you tried?" he persisted.

"I got scared and couldn't go in."

"Jael—"

"You don't know what it's like, Wallace. Don't yell at me."

"I'm not yelling. It's just so frustrating. I told you I'd go with you, and you said no. And then you didn't go either."

"You *can't* go. The meetings are just for women, and besides that, they're closed. And if you'd give me time, I'd tell you that I sat on the doorsteps during the whole thing and met a woman who's taking me with her next week so I won't feel so damned *stupid*." I set fire to one of the shavings Wallace had discarded and used it as a torch on the bottom of the stump.

"You don't have any *reason* to feel stupid," he claimed.

"Go fuck yourself," I told him. I watched the underside of the wood turn black. We didn't speak for a long time.

"I'm so scared for you," he said.

"Well, don't be," I told him sharply. "I've already lived through the hard part. There's nothing bad going on in my life right now. Nothing at all." I could feel the flame getting close to my fingers, and I liked the heat. But I blew out my torch and took up my tools again. Methodically, I chipped at the wood.

"So what's your plan?" he said quietly.

"I need to go to the river," I told him.

"Why?"

"I don't know yet."

"Are you sure?" he asked.

"I think so." I put down my wood and sniffed at my smoky hands.

"Come here," he said.

I walked over to him, and we hugged close, and I buried my nose in the place where his shoulder and neck came together.

"You have to be honest with me, you know," he whistled into my hair.

"I *am* being honest."

"I mean *really* honest. More honest than you've ever been. You have to tell me exactly how you feel."

"I already do."

"Like right now. What's going on in your head when I hold you this way?" He rocked me back and forth in his arms, and I sank into him, breathing his musky warmness.

"It feels just fine," I told him. "No lie."

I thought that the Virgin wasn't speaking to me because others were in the sanctuary. Three older women
in dresses and hats were seated in the rows of chairs
facing Jesus. But they were far away, and I was whisper-
ing. I couldn't figure out why she was being so quiet.

"Come on. Answer me," I begged as I picked the
browning leaves away from the arrangement at her feet.
"Do you think I need to tell Helen? She'll tell Arthur,
and then everybody will be upset for no good reason."

I looked up at the Virgin. She was as stony as history,
smiling down on me with the same cool lips that smiled
on every person who passed her shrine.

"I need your advice," I whispered desperately.
"Things are happening too fast. Why won't you *talk*?
They can't hear you, remember? They don't know what
to listen for."

The white lilies at her feet shuddered beneath my
touch as I brushed off each gentle leaf and blew onto
their centers. Watching them, I grew calmer. I was already kneeling, so I closed my eyes.

The white light came down on me like a warm,
transparent bubble, and I felt myself floating though I
didn't actually move.

I looked up at the Madonna. Her statue had not
changed, but I could feel her all around me, and then I
heard her speak from a place beyond her lips.

"Do you remember a time when you couldn't talk?"
she asked. "Any time at all? A time when you had so
much to say, but for one reason or another, you couldn't
make the sounds?"

"Yes," I said.

"Shhhhh. I'm telling you that you don't need your tongue to speak. All those times when you thought no one was hearing you, you weren't being ignored."

"I don't understand."

"It will come to you," she told me. "Spoken energy is no different from thought energy. Those who don't hear the thoughts usually don't hear words very well either. Listen with more than your ears and you'll be able to speak with more than your lips."

The Virgin's language eclipsed me, but being wrapped in her glow was more powerful than anything I'd felt before.

"I won't speak to you in words again," she said. "You've moved beyond that now. I'm not *in* this statue, after all. I'm in your air. And do you know the principle of the air, Jael?"

"No," I told her.

"The air teems with spirits. Whenever you breathe, you breathe them in. You can call to you whichever spirits you want. They will come to you—the peaceful ones or the anxious ones. But you have to ask for what you need. Otherwise, they don't listen."

I felt the bubble descend again and grow still.

"You won't find me here anymore," the Virgin said. "But I'll be near. Remember, you get what you ask for."

And then the bubble left me. I felt a little cold and a little empty. But I took a deep breath and thought of peaceful things, the whiteness of the lilies, the beauty of the Blessed Virgin's shrine. And though I was no longer floating, the heat of that fullness came back.

From the kitchen table, I watched Wallace make the pizza while I stretched a piece of deerskin over my hollowed stump, tacking down the edges as tautly as I could. He spread the dough across the pan, pressing out the thick places and filling in the thin ones. I found my own hands rubbing the smooth leather of my drum in anticipation.

"Wallace," I said, "will you do that to my back?"

"Do what to your back?" he asked, his face splotched with flour.

"Push on it like you're doing to that dough," I laughed.

"Do you have any idea how bad you are at flirting?" He smirked and returned to his crust. "Do you really want these hands touching you?" He had flour and stickiness all the way up to both elbows.

"I don't care."

"You asked for it." He began walking towards me like a monster, his gooey white arms held up into the air, stepping down hard on one foot and then the other.

As soon as he got close to me, I ran out of the kitchen squealing. He followed behind, his doughy hands grabbing into the air. I led him into the living room, around the sofa, down the hall, and through the back door. By the time I reached the yard, he'd almost caught up.

"Don't touch me," I teased. "You'll get that all over me." I made it to a tree and circled wide, then cut in sharp to gain some distance.

"I thought you didn't care," he joked, gaining strides.

"I changed my mind," I panted.

And then he grabbed me around the waist and took me down onto the grass. I could hardly catch my breath from all the dodging and all the laughing. He flipped me over onto my back, pinned me down, and said, "Is this what you wanted?"

"Let me up," I giggled.

"No way," he said, out of breath. "It'd be too much trouble to catch you again."

"Really, Wallace."

"Uh-uh."

"Please," I tittered. "Please let me go." I was still laughing, but fear caught in my throat. The way he held me down felt like conquest.

"I want to keep you here all night," he claimed, as he lowered himself to kiss me.

"No," I begged, but he didn't hear the panic in my voice. "Let me *up*," I screamed, and then I was shaking.

"What is it?" he asked, suddenly serious, letting go. As soon as I sat upright, I started crying.

"My God, I thought we were playing."

"We were," I whimpered.

"What happened?"

"I don't know."

He took me by the shoulders and shook me hard. "Think," he said. "Tell me when it stopped being a game for you."

But I couldn't respond. Sobs congealed in my mouth.

"When we were inside? Were you scared then?"

"That was *fun*," I blurted out.

"When we came outside?"

I shook my head.

"Was it when I grabbed you?" he asked. His face was stiff with concern, but he had horror in his eyes.

"When you held me down," I stammered. "Not until you held me down."

"I thought that was the point," he said somberly.

"It *was*."

"But I scared you."

"Not *you*," I said. "It wasn't *you*." I leaned into him. The tension in his body made his muscles feel like ropes beneath his skin.

"What was it then?"

"I was on my back," I whispered. "I thought it was another time."

I was sitting in the rocking chair, waiting for Arlene to knock and accompany me to the meeting, when the dark woman spoke up. I'd thought she was sleeping.

"Are you nervous?" she asked.

"A little," I admitted.

"Your coloring's bad."

"So's yours," I said.

"It happens that way."

My stomach felt queasy, and I thought I might have to go to the bathroom. It's nothing, I told myself. You've practically been a part of this group for months. Besides, you live here.

"Why don't you open up the hole?" the dark woman

suggested. "Then if you need to, you can look at it and see how close you are to being home."

So I pulled the sponge out of the wall. And then I stacked some books onto the floor, lifted the dark woman from the mantel, and set her there on top of them, adjusting the books until the hole in the wall framed her face.

Even though Arlene wasn't due for another five minutes, I panicked. I worried that she'd forgotten. I worried that she'd decided I wouldn't fit in with the others.

"Don't you move," I warned the dark woman.

"I won't go anywhere," she promised.

I brushed my teeth again and checked my face. I was pale.

"I'm going to wait on the doorsteps," I told her.

"You'll be fine," she assured me.

But before I could get outside, Arlene's footsteps descended to my door.

"Want an animal?" Arlene asked, dumping a box of extra stuffed animals onto the carpet. The women in the group who'd already brought toys of their own reached down and selected others.

Their laps were like zoos.

"No, thanks," I answered, smiling. I couldn't imagine myself cuddling up next to a stuffed animal—particularly in a room full of strangers. I watched their fingers kneading the soft fabric of bear backs. I held Wallace's sweatshirt in my arms, sniffed it, and brushed my nose side to side against the softness. I decided I'd rather be cold than put it on. It hung so loosely.

I recognized many of the women from the week before, but they didn't seem to recognize me. They smiled at me sympathetically, condescendingly, I thought, and I wanted to leave.

"We have a newcomer," someone noted. "Don't forget to read the 'Welcome to Newcomers.'"

And so the meeting began, as I'd heard it begin so many times before. I could almost recite the steps they read in opening.

During the moment of silence, I stole a glance at the hole in the wall where the dark woman stood guard. It appeared to be just a shadow in the distance. It seemed miles from the place where I sat.

"Hi, my name is Terri," a woman said.

"Hi, Terri," I responded with the group in perfect unison.

"Hi," she said again. "I haven't been to a meeting in a long time—almost a year. I've been doing really well with my recovery. But tonight I was in my house, in my pajamas, about to turn on the TV, and I thought about you guys and how much I missed you. So I came out tonight just to check in. And I'm really glad to have this place to return to. It feels like home."

Terri had a face full of power. Her eyes reminded me of spiderwebs, the way they dazzled.

"And that's all I need to say," she explained. "I pass."

The silence between speakers had never felt so palpable from the other side of the wall. It was all I could do to stay in that room while no one was speaking. I thought about how many people considered that place their home. It was so close to *my* home. So near.

"Hi, I'm Olivia," another woman said.

"Hi, Olivia," I repeated, my voice blending with others of different pitches.

"I had something very upsetting happen," she stammered, and then the tears began.

Someone picked up the pink box of tissues from the coffee table and passed them to her. I could not watch her cry. It seemed like betrayal. Another woman across the room grew misty-eyed. I lowered my head and thought of the serenity prayer. I could think of a thousand dryer ways to mourn the pain.

"I had to leave my husband this week," she said quietly, but her voice grew louder and louder as she continued. "Because I found out he's been molesting my little girl."

And then she broke into loud, soulful wailing. I had never heard a woman cry that way. All her lungs, all her throat joined in the endeavor. It was a noise that reduced me to elements.

"I hadn't even *noticed*," she bawled, "as well as I knew the signs."

I looked to the place where the dark woman waited. I have to leave, I thought to her. I can't listen to this.

"It belongs to you, too," the dark woman's voice echoed in my head. "Stay with it."

All around the room, the women kept their heads bowed in respect for Olivia's pain. And Arlene, who sat next to her, wrapped her arms around the woman as she shook and moaned out her guilt, her fury, her sadness.

Her weeping hazed over the air. I could crouch beneath it, I thought. If I could get low enough to the ground, I wouldn't have to feel it.

I saw the white light slip into the room through the hole in the wall. She lit up the entire room with her glow.

"Go *to* her," I screamed in my head, thinking that the Virgin's spirit wouldn't hear me for all the crying.

"She isn't ready yet," the white light answered.

"Can't you do anything?" I begged.

"There's a time for this sort of passion, Jael," she answered. "Olivia is in the right place to exorcise these feelings."

"Well, what are you doing here, then?" I asked. Her glowing figure stood directly before me. The other women in the room didn't seem to notice at all.

"I'm here for *you*," she answered. "*You're* the one who called. Breathe."

I inhaled deeply and pulled her spirit into my lungs. The whole place turned fuzzy. I was warm, and I thought I might lift off.

"What can I do to help her?" I asked the white light.

"Just stay," the light said. It spoke in my voice.

There is nothing so beautiful and haunting as the sound of a woman crying. The low notes stretched out and holding, declining. The rapid intake of air. The spontaneity of it. The sighing. The moan that rises up from her round belly, through her round chest, can only come out round. Woman cries in circles. And if her sobs are broken, they're no less resonant. Weeping is a song of shudders harmonizing with bursts of wails. When a woman cries, even the dust in the air trembles.

In the night I heard someone sob, and I thought Olivia had returned to the next room to complete her grieving. I knew I should go to her and sit with her, but I couldn't rouse myself.

I could feel my own bed shaking with the intensity of her sorrow. Again and again, the long lamenting cries broke into my sleep like wind thrashing through the trees during a storm.

In the distance, I could hear the dark woman and the white light speaking. It had awakened them, too.

"It's hard to leave her this way," the dark woman whispered.

"It's for her own good," the white light replied.

I couldn't talk with Helen just anywhere. It seemed important to have her grounded with my kind of reality when I explained to her that I remembered everything about my past. So I'd called her up, told her I needed to meet with her, and asked if she minded speaking with me in the woods. When she arrived at the church, I was waiting for her on my doorsteps. "Come on," I called, motioning her to the trees.

"Are the snakes crawling yet?" she asked.

"Saw one the other day," I laughed. "Don't worry. I'll lead."

We passed through the maze of trees, kicking up mulch, crunching lichen, and hiking in deeper and deeper.

"You sure you know how to get out of here?" Helen asked.

"Yep," I told her. "Watch out for that root."

We walked until we came to the tangle of briers where Magdelena, the woman I'd met at the Laundromat back in autumn, had led me to the stream. I hadn't been to the stream since that night. It had seemed so magical, so fated, that I'd been scared it hadn't been real. But it seemed like the perfect place for an unveiling. I pushed through the briers, held them back for Helen, and moved on in.

"I don't think we're going to be able to get through, Jael."

"Yes, we are," I assured her. "Step up high over that one."

Past the briers, once again, we came to the enchanted place where crape myrtles with their peeling bark obscured the shiny stream.

"We're almost there," I told her, and then the stream came into view.

"My God," Helen exclaimed. "This is lovely. Does Arthur know this place is down here?"

"Don't know," I said. "You can sit on that bent tree if you want, but I think the ground is dry."

She found a place to roost, and I reclined on the earth's floor.

"So why have you brought me here?" she asked, her brow sweaty in spite of the day's tendency towards briskness.

"Well," I started, "I haven't been up front with you exactly—about the things I remember—about my past."

"Mmm-hhhmmm."

"I mean, I know where I came from—besides the river. Did you know that already?"

Helen paused, pulled her lips to one side. "Not at first," she said. "When you were in the hospital and even after you'd started working at the church, I thought I was dealing with a full-blown case of amnesia. But after a while, I noticed that you weren't particularly worried about remembering. With amnesia, most patients work very hard to recover their memories. They get frustrated that they can't remember their pasts. They visit places that they think might help them recall something. They make lists of things they're good and bad at. And they're under a different kind of stress than you've exhibited. So I figured out a good while back that whatever you had going on in your hard head was something besides amnesia." She looked over at me and smiled. Her eyes became slits in her round face. "Are you going to tell me the real story?"

I could see a crawdaddy sitting on the bottom of the stream. What I wouldn't give to be you, I thought. Hidden down there out of everybody's way. Reaching into the water, I picked up a little rock. I tossed it near the crawdaddy and watched him scamper farther upstream.

"I heard it sink," Helen said.

"You *did*?"

"I think so."

"Helen, I'm not sure I can tell you."

"You still have trouble trusting me?"

"No, no," I reassured her. "It isn't that. It's just that—well—I don't know where to start."

"Take your time and begin wherever it feels natural."

So beneath the crape myrtles and beside the stream, I told Helen the same things I'd told Wallace—how I'd been hurt by some of the men at Mammie's store, how when she died I left there and went to live with River Bill, how that relationship became more than I'd expected, and how I'd left with Thompie Hayes. I explained that living off the land was nothing new to me, and that staying by the river alone for all that time was both the thing that saved me and the thing that made me ill. When I was done, Helen's eyes were cloudy, and she looked at me in a way I hadn't seen before.

"I didn't mean to lie, exactly," I explained. "But I knew that if I told you the place I was from, you'd send me there again."

Helen lifted her weight from the bent-over tree and sat down near me on the ground.

"Do you ever cry about it?" she asked.

"Sometimes," I said. "Why?"

"Because you deliver that story like it's rehearsed, like you've repeated it to yourself so many times that you don't feel it anymore."

"Of course I feel it."

"Really?" she asked, her eyes filling again.

The sight of Helen crying was more than I'd anticipated. I didn't know how to react, and it made me uncomfortable to think that my words had affected her so strongly. She seemed to sense my stirrings, said, "It's okay. You have no idea what an emotional person you're speaking to. Keep going." She took my hand, squeezed it. Her hand was cold.

I didn't have anything else to say. It seemed like

something else was there, but then it was gone before I could remember.

"I don't know what else to say," I told her.

"Tell me when you *feel* it."

It struck me as a ridiculous request. It wasn't the kind of thing I could touch. "I feel it when the moon holds its water," I told her, for lack of a better answer.

"What?"

"It's something Mammie used to say. When the moon was waxing and it looked like a big grin in the sky, Mammie would tell me that the moon was holding its water. She said it did it for spite, said it couldn't rain until the moon tipped enough to spill the water out. I *never* saw the moon turned up like a basin during rain. So I thought Mammie was magic. I thought she knew everything."

Helen said, "Hmmm," and nodded her head. We sat that way for a long time, trying to make meaning of the world, I guess.

"It was just one of her sayings," I continued. "But at some point I realized that any time it *wasn't* raining, the moon must be holding its water. The rain was only occasional. I remember thinking about how it felt to hold my own water, how uncomfortable and even painful if I waited too long. I used to feel sorry for the moon when it was turned that way—like it couldn't help itself."

I wasn't sure what I was saying made sense. It didn't make sense to me, but somehow it explained things.

"And then one day, I learned about the phases of the moon. The moon grins every single month. And when it's rainy, you can't see the moon for the clouds, no matter how it's shaped. I know the moon has power, but it's a different kind—"

Helen didn't say anything, so I kept talking.

"There's this room next to my apartment where these women have incest survivor meetings every Wednesday night. I've been going."

"Good," she said. "I didn't know that."

"So I feel it there," I told her. I picked up a stick and started scratching my name into the ground. "And sometimes when I'm with Wallace . . ."

"What's that like?"

"Usually, it's good. But sometimes, I see things—or even hear things from a long time ago."

"When does it happen?"

"Helen—"

"No, I'm serious. I need to know. Is it when you're being sexual?"

Being sexual. It sounded so ugly. I glanced at her quickly to try to read her face. I was afraid, for just a moment, that she might be laughing, but she wasn't.

"Yeah," I admitted. "I feel it *then*."

"That's pretty standard for sexual abuse victims in general."

Sexual abuse *survivors,* I thought. That's what I'd heard in the group. We were no longer victims, we were survivors. Who cares, I thought. It *all* sounded clinical. Another language of oppression. Victims, survivors, robots. I pulled off my boot and sock, doused my foot in the water, splashing back and forth. I wasn't sure I should have told her. Now I'd probably have to talk about it every week.

"I'm glad you told me," Helen said. "I hope you feel

safe about it. I hope you trust me enough to know that I won't break confidences."

"But you'll tell Arthur, right?"

She looked almost hurt. "No. I won't tell anyone at all. Not without your permission."

"Good," I said, knowing that I sounded as though I was making light of my recent disclosures, "because I don't want Arthur to know. It'd make things uncomfortable."

"Are you *scared* of him, Jael?"

"No."

"I won't say a word."

But that's not the only way to communicate, I thought. I wondered if Helen knew.

We sat in silence for a few more minutes.

"I came here once before with a woman I met at the Laundromat," I told her.

"Really?"

"I think she was crazy," I said. "But she wanted to show me the moon. It was low that night."

On our walk back to the church, I felt more sad and more angry than usual. And I also felt threatened. Only weeks earlier, my secrets had been all mine. Then something had made me tell. First Wallace, then Helen. And those women from the meeting. Though they didn't know any specifics, they all knew what I'd discovered to be the single most controlling aspect of my life.

I felt sort of like a dinosaur bone, hidden in the earth for millions of years—then stumbled across by an archaeologist on a regular afternoon and on the evening news that very night.

I stood naked in front of my mirror and looked at myself. It made me laugh, the way the scars marked my body in every direction. "What was I *thinking*?" I asked the dark woman. "Check this out. I tried to tattoo myself with berries and pine needles and some of it actually worked." I showed her the bluish dots on my arm.

"You were doing what you needed to do then. Claiming yourself. It wasn't a bad thing."

"I don't think they look like flaws anymore," I told her. "They look more like—like scars." I laughed. "See here where I carved my name?"

"You ever feel like cutting at yourself anymore?"

"I don't think so. I haven't done it in a while."

"It was a stage," the dark woman sighed. "People go through them all the time." Her mossy hair stood out all over her head. "Like me. I'm a stage for you right now. You use me while you need me, and then you move on to something else," she said in her ho-hum way.

"I'm not going to leave you," I said, turning to her naked.

"Sure you will," she said. "But do you remember what you were feeling when you slashed yourself up?"

"Yeah."

"Well, when I'm gone, you'll remember what you felt when we had our little talks. I don't know what you're whining about anyway. You never especially liked me."

"I like you," I insisted. "I just think you're nasty sometimes."

"Whatever," she said.

"Where are you going?" I asked.

"Wherever you take me," she said.

"I'm not taking you anywhere. I'm leaving your mean little body right on that mantel," I joked.

I paraded in front of the mirror a bit longer, inspecting myself. My hips were growing wider, and my breasts had gotten round since the sickness had left me and I'd gone to work at the church. Even the big jagged scar above my belly seemed to have faded into me a bit. I liked the way it sat up on top of my skin. I definitely looked like a woman. A woman I'd designed.

When my drum was completely finished, the skin tight across the wood, the wood oiled and sweet, Wallace dug a hole in his backyard, lined it with smooth rocks, and proceeded to build a fire.

"That'll work better if you make a little tepee with those sticks instead of just stacking them."

"I've always done it this way," he claimed. "I was a Boy Scout, you know."

"I *didn't* know. But I'm telling you that I've built a lot of fires, and it's going to take twice as long doing it your way."

"Fine," Wallace said, standing up. "*You* build the fire. I'll go upstairs and bring down a couple of the craft show chairs. We'll smudge them up a little—give them that authentic look."

I hurried to get the fire started quickly, and began beating on my drum as soon as I'd finished to let him know the task was done. When he came out with the stubby wooden chairs beneath each arm, I was beating the deerskin irregularly and singing, *"Booohh, baa-deeeeeee. Booh, booh, booh baa-deeee."*

He looked at the small flames curling greedy around the sticks. "Remarkable," he said.

In the chairs we sat so low to the ground that we appeared to be squatting. We sat on opposite sides of the fire, the flames blazing between us. I held the drum between my legs and pounded out a rhythm in the duskiness.

Wallace closed his eyes and began humming. As soon as his voice came in, I lost the beat and started laughing.

"Sorry," I giggled. "Let's try it again."

I repositioned my drum, dragged my hand across the skin, and tapped with my thumbs a *hard,* soft, soft, soft, *hard,* soft, soft, soft. I told myself not to look up and not to listen to anything besides the vibrations of the drum. I noticed when Wallace began to sing, but I did not break my pounding.

The song changed into different songs as my hands moved faster. Occasionally, I'd miss a beat, but I kept playing and Wallace hummed his throaty sounds into the night.

"Drum solo," I yelled, and Wallace hushed as I smacked every part of that instrument, throwing my neck and shoulders into it, too. Towards the end, I couldn't find any beat at all and just seemed to be knocking my palms against the smooth skin.

"I think it's over," Wallace said.

"No, it's not. This is a bridge into a new song," I laughed.

"Oh, Lord," he moaned.

I peeked up long enough to catch his eye, see him shake his head and smile. I knew I looked wild to him, throwing my hair all around, and I didn't want to stop. I wanted to see how far I could go.

"Oh-hh-hh-hh-hhhhhh, oh, oh, oh, oh," I sang, my voice going lower and lower, and I beat the drum and swayed in my squatting chair.

"Uhhmmm," he sighed.

I stood up, packed the drum beneath my arm, and began dancing around the fire as I thumped out the rhythm.

"You're going to have to practice," Wallace said.

"What do you mean?" I asked, continuing my procession.

"I mean that you can't hold a beat worth a damn," he laughed.

"Well *you* play it," I suggested, and I tossed him the drum over the flames.

"For one thing, the skin needs tightening." He held the drum towards the fire and let it get warm.

"Come on," I told him. "I feel like dancing."

So Wallace pounded at the drum, and it spoke to him as though it were an old friend. When I first started dancing, I was just playing, but then the beat got to me, got in me, and I liked moving that way. I didn't want to stop. I arched my body and slithered my hips as I stepped around the fire, listening to the music and watching the embers spit up at the dark sky.

After a while, I got sweaty and hot, and danced away from the fire. I backed over to a tree, put my hands on the trunk, and stroked it like a lover as my body moved. I held the trunk between my knees, threw my head back, and felt the pounding shiver through my thighs.

Wallace began humming to his own quick rhythm. I started singing too, and I twisted my way to where he sat, stood behind him, my legs embracing his back, and I swayed harder.

Our shadow was big and kinetic.

Wallace put the drum down.

In his lap, I hummed the same song into his mouth, locked my ankles around his back, and felt the beat still coursing through my body.

Only once did the familiar "Hi, my name is River Bill" distract me from the rhythm.

"Wallace," I called out.

"It's me," he said.

And the firelight at my back lit up his face and proved him right.

~~~

Arlene ordered coffee again, but I asked for a milk shake instead.

"Tough meeting," she said. "Seems like the last couple have been pretty rough. Usually they aren't so intense."

"Yeah," I answered knowingly.

"I don't know your experiences," Arlene began, "but I just want to make sure you understand that it doesn't matter how severe the abuse was. I mean, we don't rank incest. Do you see what I'm getting at?"

"Not exactly."

"Well, I'll just come right out with it. You haven't spoken in the meetings, and maybe you just haven't felt comfortable enough with us yet. It can take some time. But since you've started coming, it seems like we've heard some pretty powerful stories—the child-molester husband, and all that ritual abuse stuff. So I wanted to make sure you know that even if you don't have any memories yet, you're in the right place. You wouldn't choose to spend your evenings with incest survivors if you didn't have an important reason."

"Yeah." I nodded, even though I wasn't sure I agreed.

"It's been hard for me sometimes—when I hear these women who've been prostituted by their fathers or whatever—to accept my own abuse as valid. I beat myself up about it, you know? I'll say, 'Oh, Arlene, you're blowing things out of proportion. Nothing ever happened to you except that your big brother held you down and kissed you.' But then I think about what an impact it had on my life. And how my brother, goddamn him, wasn't thinking about anybody but himself. He didn't care that I was a sexual person with feelings that were getting more and more confused. He didn't listen when I begged him to stop. And even though nobody put their hands down my pants, I ended up with the same hang-ups as the people who were victimized by these child-pornography rings. You see what I'm getting at?"

"Mmm-hhhmmm." I sucked on my straw.

"And I'll tell you another thing," Arlene continued. She was getting wound up. "Whenever you think that you're exaggerating a memory or a situation, you just remember whose side you're on. The abusers will *always* tell you you're exaggerating. Do you know why? Because they're so caught up in what *they* want, that they can't admit in their seedy little hearts that they've got the capacity to hurt somebody else. Stupid asses. And if you believe them, you betray yourself. You gotta listen to what's in here," and she thumped her chest.

I smiled at her. She was beautiful the way fruit is beautiful. "Thanks," I said. She was trying to help.

But the one thing I knew for certain was that all pains were not equal. A kiss, no matter how tormenting, was not a fuck. While I was sorry Arlene still hurt inside, a part of me wanted to tell her to count her blessings, to tell them *all* to count their blessings. We might have been hurt, but we were still alive. We were staring at an invitation to keep living, too angry to even notice.

I wondered if maybe Arlene had been in the group too long.

"You doing okay?" she asked me.

"Yeah."

"I didn't mean to go on and on like that."

"It's good for me to hear you," I told her. "I'm new at this. I'll have more to say when I get it all . . . figured out."

"Honey, when you get it figured out, make sure you fill me in," she laughed. "You in a hurry?"

"No."

"Do you care if I have some pie? Whenever I start mouthing off about this, I crave sweets."

"Go ahead."

Arlene held up her hand and waved it at the waiter. Her silver bracelets tinkled together like a wind chime. He came to our table and she ordered.

"You want some?" she asked.

"No, thanks."

"That's all then," she said to the waiter, and he left.

"So what's going on with you?"

I wondered what sort of question she was asking. I thought she probably meant to stay with the subject of the meeting, but I was ready to change it. "I'm going on vacation," I told her. "Next week."

"Really?" she asked. "Where you going?"

"Camping at the river."

"With friends?"

"Just my friend Wallace."

"Is he a regular friend or a special one?" she asked.

"He's a pretty special one," I said, grinning, and since I knew that I was grinning, I blushed.

"Oh," she said. "Sounds fun."

I dreamed that I was taking a walk through the woods, and suddenly the pollen started falling lightly out of the trees. Then it fell harder and harder until it poured, covering the ground like snow. I was to my knees in pollen, and I could see that up ahead, it had settled into big drifts. The wind blew and pollen swarmed around in the air.

"There are no trees in the river. Go there," I heard

a voice say, and I knew it was the dark woman even though I couldn't see her.

"Where are you?" I called, but pollen filled my mouth.

"Not out in that mess. That's for sure," she said. "Go towards the river. You're almost there."

I was wading through, barely able to move.

I couldn't see anymore, and I could hardly breathe.

Then the white light appeared in the distance, and she lit up the way. I could see the river behind her, and I trudged in that direction. I could see the glow of her gesturing arms calling me.

I'm not going to make it, I thought.

She reached her hands towards me, and I reached for the light. It pulled me through the air and straight into the water.

Part Three

I pulled on my blue jeans and a sweatshirt, tied my hair back in a bandana, and tugged on the new hiking boots I'd bought especially for the occasion. I'd already packed my change of clothes and a sketchpad and pens into the backpack that Wallace had loaned me. The only thing left to do was wait for the battered station wagon to arrive.

The phone rang. I hurried to turn down the radio and answered it.

"Jael?" she said.

"Hi, Helen."

"I'm glad I caught you before you left. Is Wallace there?"

"Not yet."

"Well, I called to tell you to have a good trip. I'll be thinking about you."

"Thanks."

"Be prepared for some strong emotions. You've got all sorts of feelings tied up in that place."

"I think I'm ready," I told her.

"You're in good hands with Wallace. Are you ex-cited?"

"Pretty much, yeah. He's late."

"You can call me, you know, if you need to."

"I might have to hike out a ways—to get to a tele-phone."

"Well, that's been done before," she said. "I'll see you in a week."

"Okay, thanks for calling."

As soon as I'd said good-bye to Helen, someone knocked at my door. I knew it wasn't Wallace because his car had a loud muffler, and I would have heard him drive up. Besides, he always knocked on the wood, and this person used the knocker.

When I opened the door, Arthur stood there in his little black suit, his glasses cocked the tiniest bit side-ways.

"Father," I said, "come in." Arthur hadn't been in my apartment since I'd first moved in. I could tell that he was looking around, inspecting the way I'd decorated the place, probably wondering where I slept and why there were sticks leaning in corners. If I'd known he was coming, I would have dusted.

"Sit down," I said.

"I can't stay," he replied, but he settled into my rocking chair. "Wallace isn't here yet?"

"I'm expecting him any minute," I told him.

"Good, good."

"Can I get you something to drink?" I offered, think-ing that I'd already finished off the milk and the juice. There was nothing but water.

"No. I just stopped by to tell you to have a wonderful vacation."

"Thanks," I said. "I'm planning to." I heard the

rumble of the station wagon pull up outside and then the ignition cut off.

"Jael," Arthur said, "I must admit that I can't quite figure you out. I don't know what it is that you're working through, but I want you to know that I'll support you—whatever it is."

I felt the color climb into my cheeks.

"I want you to take this with you—on your trip." He handed me a fifty-dollar bill folded tightly into a tiny rectangle, and his face turned as red as mine.

"Jael," Wallace called from outside and then tapped at the door.

"Thank you so much," I said, "but I can't take your money."

"It's a bonus. For your good work. Please—"

I ran over to the door and opened it for Wallace. He seemed surprised to see Arthur standing there, maybe because we both looked like lobsters with our pink complexions.

"Father Burke," Wallace said.

"How are you, Wallace?"

They shook hands.

"I just came by to give this adventure my blessings," Arthur announced. "Vacations are good for the soul. May you find the promised land." He grinned at himself for a moment, then stopped. "Seriously," he said, "have a good trip."

"Yes, sir." Wallace saluted.

I led Arthur to the door. "Thank you, Father," I whispered, and I gave him an awkward one-armed hug.

He nodded once more to Wallace and closed the door behind him.

"That was strange," Wallace said.

"Sweet," I told him. "He brought me a gift."

We loaded my backpack into the car, along with the tent, the groceries, and Wallace's belongings.

"You sure you have everything?" Wallace asked.

"Got it," I said.

He cranked the car and pulled out towards the road.

"Wait," I yelled. "There's one thing."

I ran back into my apartment, grabbed the dark woman under my arm, and bolted back out to the place where Wallace was waiting.

I'd called the hospital and then the rescue squad, looking for the exact location where I'd been taken from the woods into the city. So we knew the vicinity, but not the spot. Wallace had marked the area on the map, and I held it in my hands, calling out turns and road numbers.

We drove out of the city and into the country, where only local convenience stores and pastures dotted the roadsides, an occasional house or barn.

"How does it feel?" Wallace asked.

"Like nothing special," I told him. "I've never seen this place in my life—at least not that I can remember."

We stopped, got gas, and continued on our journey.

"We should be in the right area," Wallace said. "Are any of these dirt roads on the map?"

"Not that I can tell," I told him. "There's one coming up soon with a number."

He pulled off the road, took the map from me, and said, "We're close, and the river's over there. I think we should just take one of these small roads and see where we end up. If nothing else, we can find a place to camp for the night and try again in the morning."

"Sounds good," I said. We had a whole week to look for my river spot. I knew we'd find it, though I didn't know why. "Let's consult the dark woman," I said, and placed her on the dashboard. I arranged her tangled hair, wiped her eyes clear with my thumbs, and asked, "Which way should we go."

She didn't answer, of course.

"What'd she say?" Wallace played along.

"She says you're right," I told him. "Turn at the very next one."

We made our way down a single-laned sandy road. We rounded deep curves and passed over little bridges as we got closer and closer to the river. Finally, the road came to an end. Wallace stopped the car in a clearing no bigger than a small parking lot.

"Let's make camp," he said.

With flashlights, we surveyed the area. There were weeds and bushes all over the place. The smoothest surface for pitching the tent seemed to be down near the river, on the sand.

"Let's put it there," I told Wallace.

"Hmmm, I've never pitched a tent in sand. Won't the pins pull out?"

"Trust me," I told him. "Could you get me that pot out of the car?"

"What for?" he asked.

"For water," I told him.

He didn't ask any more questions, and pulled the gear out of the car while I went to the river, scooped up water, and poured it on the ground. When I was finished, I filled the pot one last time and drank hard. I had not lost my appreciation for the taste.

"Now the pins will hold," I told him. "The sand's packed."

I built a fire. He raised the tent. Over the flame, we cooked beans.

Later when we had tucked ourselves beneath a sleeping bag, he asked me what it was like, knowing that I was near the place where Thompie Hayes had left me.

"Sort of scary," I told him.

"I can't imagine what sort of fool would want to leave you." He reached to rub my head but hit my nose instead.

I knew Wallace was tired. I could hear his breathing slow down and deepen. But I was wide awake.

"It feels like ages since I was here," I said, "but it's only been a year. Isn't that strange?"

"Mmm-hhhmmm," he groaned and rolled over.

All around me the river noises amplified in my ears. There was a certain thrill in being so close to the water.

As soon as I knew Wallace was sleeping, I pulled away from him, unzipped the tent, and tiptoed out into the moist night air.

A chorus of crickets welcomed me back.

I dipped my toes into the water and stirred up the minnows even though I couldn't see them.

I stretched out on the dry river sand and looked up at the dimly lit sky. Clouds obscured the moon and then passed on, blotting out stars a few at a time, shadowlike. Moss draped from the old oak trees at the river's edge. I imagined what sort of spirits were around me, all the drowned ones pulling themselves up from the slick muddy bottom and out into the night.

"Hello, out there," I whispered to them. "I know you hear me. I'm sleeping here tonight. Watch over me."

The sand was grainy and light. I rolled in it like a cat, thrilled with the texture. Then I curled up on my side and inhaled the river spirits.

The next morning, we broke camp and drove back to the main road the way we'd come. Wallace wanted to go into the nearest town and try to rent a boat. I told him that you couldn't rent boats—not out in the country, but he said, "If there's a will, there's a way."

In the daylight, the bridges looked particularly rickety. But the whole swampy area had greened with the season, and through the morning's haze, the place appeared enchanted and familiar.

Wallace kept looking at me and at the woods and back at me again. "Incredible," he said.

"Sure is," I agreed.

When we were almost to the main road again, we came upon a truck with a boat attached. The driver pulled off to the side of the road to let us pass. As we approached, he waved as though he knew us.

"Friendly guy," Wallace said. "Let's see if he knows where we can rent a boat."

"Wallace," I said, embarrassed, and I sank my head into my hands as I heard him roll down the window and pull up next to the truck.

"How you doing?" the man in the truck asked. He had his cap pulled down low on his head, and his words were thickened by the chewing tobacco that made his face appear swollen on one side. He could have been one of the members of River Bill's church, but I knew we were far from that place.

"Good, thanks," Wallace answered. "We're on vacation down here—wondering if you know anywhere we could rent a boat."

The man looked up to the ceiling of his pickup as if the answer was written there, shook his head a couple of times, and said, "Ain't never heard of nobody *renting* a boat and motor. You might could *borry* one from somebody." Then he spit out the truck window.

Wallace laughed. "Afraid we don't know anyone in these parts."

"Hey," I yelled over Wallace. "You don't by any chance remember a woman getting rescued down here—about a year ago—do you?"

The man looked up again, scratched his nose, and said, "There was a wild girl, went crazy, had to be tooken to the crazy house. I reckon that was about a year ago. Is 'at who you mean?"

"Maybe so," I said. "You know where they found her?"

"I believe she was over near Bitterroot Landing."

"Can you tell us how to get there?" Wallace asked.

"I don't think you can get there in *that*," he said, pointing to the station wagon. "You'll bog down."

"We can hike in," Wallace said.

"I reckon you can if you want to, but it's a loooong way to walk."

"That's okay."

"Go on out to the main road," the man said, "and take a left. You'll drive about five miles down that road before you come to a hog farm on the right. There's a dirt road to the left. You turn there. Then you follow that road a long way till you come to a fork in it. You take a right, and then follow it out till you can't drive no more." The man hawked and spit. "Don't you try to put that car through them bogs," he said. "Won't nobody know you in there, and it might be a week 'fore you get out."

"Thanks a lot," Wallace said.

The man nodded and drove on.

"Ever heard of Bitterroot Landing?" Wallace asked.

"No," I said.

"I think we better double-check those directions in town."

"What are we going to town for?" I asked.

"To see if we can rent a boat."

"You can't *rent* boats in the country, Wallace," I told him again.

"Let's just see," he said.

We were sitting in a parking lot eating burgers and fries. I was so mad at Wallace I could hardly swallow anymore. I drained the rest of my drink loudly. "Can we just *go*?" I asked him. It was lunchtime, and we'd spent the entire morning driving around, talking with farmers and fishermen, looking for a place to rent a boat.

Wallace pissed me off, acting like he enjoyed getting to know the country people even though he knew it was people just like them who mistreated me.

"We've got six days, Jael. Calm down."

"I've been calm all morning," I told him. "But you don't listen to anything I tell you, and it makes me *crazy*. I grew up in a place like this. I *know* you can't just go rent a boat, and I've told you that ten thousand times. If you want one so bad, why don't you *buy* a damned boat?"

"We're doing this for you, remember?"

"We don't need a boat," I told him. "I'm not getting in a boat even if you find one."

"Gratitude," Wallace muttered and then he got mad with me. "You're acting like a goddamned baby. Why don't you just set yourself on fire, Jael? That's what people in Korea do when *they* get angry about something."

"Piss off," I told him. "And don't give me your gratitude shit, either. I know what I need, and you just *think* you know. You get in a boat on this river, and you never know *where* you might wind up." I bent over and turned on the radio.

"Oh," Wallace said, and his face changed from annoyed to serene.

"Besides that, just how do you plan to get the boat you rent to the river, anyway? We already know that we can't drive there. Are we going to pull the boat behind us? Do you have any idea how much a boat weighs?"

"You're scared you're going to see him, aren't you?"

"You've probably never been in a boat in your life—stupid, city-assed . . ."

"You're scared you're going to see him," he said again, quieter.

"Who?"

"River Bill."

"I am *not* going to see him," I yelled. "I just want to get to the river." I was worked up and anxious. The food settled hard in my stomach. I wasn't acting like myself.

"Okay, okay," Wallace said. He smiled at me, took my hand, and said, "We'll do it your way."

I yanked my hand out of his, said, "I don't *care* whose way we do it."

I went into the bathroom and started crying. Wallace made me crazy, not hearing me. I plopped down on the toilet and wrapped toilet tissue around my hand. I was sad.

In Korea, students set themselves on fire to make other people *listen*. It didn't require any words at all. "I'm unhappy," they stated, their torch-hands blazing pain into the air. "Pay attention," they demanded, their lips bubbling up, tarry. "This is what oppression smells like."

Their friends could not cry enough to extinguish the flames. I wondered if Wallace could.

I wondered what would happen if my therapy group set itself on fire. If we dipped our clothes in gasoline and lit a single match, passing it from hand to hand.

"Hi, I'm Arlene. I'm an incest survivor."

Poof. " 'Bye, Arlene."

"Hi, I'm Jael."

Poof. " 'Bye, Jael."

And then we would be a circle of fire, an irregular circle of fire. And in the center, the pink box of Kleenex would go unworshipped.

I wondered how it would feel to hold the fiery hands of my baby-fucked sisters, chanting, "Don't fuck your babies. Don't fuck your sisters," until we sizzled and singed and melted together.

I imagined we would give off an incredible light.

And we would howl. We would smolder for a millennium.

When we couldn't drive any farther, Wallace pulled the car off the side of the road, and we opened the back and began loading our packs.

"What do you think?" he said cheerfully. "Should we take all the supplies or just part of them?"

"As much as we can carry," I said. "We'll be staying for a while."

"Does this place look familiar?"

"No. But it feels right."

My pack was full, but Wallace's had room.

"You want to take her?" he asked, pointing to the dark woman still sitting in the front seat.

"Yeah," I said.

Wallace leaned over the seat and grabbed her while I unzipped my gear and pulled out a lantern.

"You carry this," I told him. "She needs to ride with me."

We set out on foot through the swampland, and Wallace led the way.

"You know what to do if you see an alligator, don't you?" I half-joked.

"Are you serious?"

"Well, we're in the swamp." I shrugged.

"What?" he asked.

"Throw your pack at it, and run the other way."

"That makes sense," he said.

"Or climb a tree," I told him. "It takes an alligator a while to climb a tree."

The road thickened up again, and we walked side by side without saying much. There was a certain stillness, a solemnity in the air, knowing that no one was going to pass us. After a while, we stopped, drank water, rested on the ground. When we resumed our pace, I grabbed his hand.

"You okay?" he asked.

"A little nervous," I told him. "A little shaky but excited. Except sometimes I get scared that the place I remember doesn't exist."

"You think you made it up?"

"No, I don't think so. It's just really important to

find it because sometimes it's hard for me to keep straight what happened in real life and what happened in my mind. Like—I wonder sometimes if I lived beneath that tree for as long as I think I did. I wonder if maybe I was only there for one night and maybe everything else that I remember was a hallucination or something."

"Hmmm," he said, and adjusted his pack.

"It's all tied together," I told him. "Like when I have memories and flashbacks and dreams. They're all different, and then I can't remember how it actually happened. You know?"

"I think so," he said. "But do you think it matters?"

"What do you mean?"

"Does it make any difference what really happened? I mean, if you have a flashback that scares you, whether or not it happened the way you remember it, you're still scared, right?"

"Yeah."

"So why would it matter whether your memories are accurate?"

"Because if the memories aren't real, then maybe I'm not either." Sometimes Wallace acted like such a *man*, but I forgave him.

We were so deep in conversation that we walked up on a long black snake stretched out across the road, sunning itself.

"Snake," I screamed, and Wallace jumped back.

There was swamp on either side of us, and the lazy reptile seemed to have no intention of making our passage any easier. I was carrying a long stick that I'd picked up along the way. The dark woman said, "Poke him with the stick. He'll move."

I'm scared of snakes, I thought.

"Just poke him gently," she demanded.

"Back up," I said to Wallace.

"What are you doing?" he asked.

I took the stick and nudged the snake's tail. "We're not going to hurt you," I whispered.

"Be careful," Wallace said.

It slithered off into the swamp.

"Gross," I grunted.

"You just take control of things, don't you?"

"Better keep your eyes peeled for the kind that like to drop out of trees," I told him.

We came to a place where the road turned into a path, and the tree branches on either side locked their limbs together to form a thick wood awning.

"Ever seen this before?" Wallace asked, ducking.

"I don't think so," I told him.

"Seems like you'd remember."

We passed beneath the twining trees. It was like walking into another world. I almost expected Mariah to walk out and greet me. Or wood nymphs. The bushes were thick, and though the path was still evident, we had to stomp down all sorts of wild tangles.

"So what I was saying, Jael, is that it shouldn't matter to you if you don't find this particular tree that you slept under. Because whether we find it or not, it's real to you."

"But it isn't real to *you* yet," I told him. "And I'm going to take you there."

~~~

We wound up at the place where Thompie Hayes and I had spent the night. The tiny camper was still there and also the sign in the window that said LIAR'S JUNCTION. When I saw it, I squealed out, threw down my backpack, and ran to the river. It was late afternoon and we were tired, but inside I felt like morning. I felt like the world had just been created, and it was all mine.

Wallace burst into laughter, watching me strip off my clothes and splash out into the water. "I take it that you know this place?" he called.

"Oh, *yeah*," I said.

"Welcome home."

He unlaced his boots and began to shed his own clothes. I stood in the river, submerged to my waist, and watched him begin his descent.

"Whoa, it's cold."

"What'd you expect?" I giggled. "Come on."

We rinsed each other in the water, teeth chattering but happy.

"Who does the trailer belong to?" he asked.

"Don't know," I said. I sank under, filled my mouth, and then squirted water through the air in a little arc.

"Did you stay here before?" he asked.

"Not for long," I told him. "But I know where I am. I wasn't wrong."

We camped there that night but didn't bother with the tent.

"I need to sleep on the ground," I told Wallace. "With you."

"Jael," he started.

"Please," I said. "I need to sleep in the sand, and when I wake up, I need you to be here."

"I'll be here," he assured me.

I sat the dark woman on a stump near the camper, and she watched us while we rested. Once, I woke up, felt the man sleeping beside me, his chin sunk into my breasts, and I stroked his hair, said, "Wallace?"

"I'm here," he whispered.

And I saw the white light rise up from the river, so I knew it was safe to close my eyes again.

At dawn when the river was still and the darkness prepared to give itself over to its warm shadow, I woke up. Wallace slept quiet beside me. I ran my hand through the sand, sifted it through my fingers, felt the grains falling individually back to the earth.

Though I didn't know exactly who to pray to, I knew I needed to pray. With my eyes wide open, I thanked the spirits for leading me to the place I needed to be.

And then as the moon turned into the sun right before my eyes, I watched things become their opposites. The dark woman became light, and the white light rose dark from the water. The earth beneath me grew buoyant as time, and the river turned solid as life.

The morning told me a story that had no words, but I heard it anyway. It was a tale about a woman who was lost on the river-sea, and she floated on a dead fish. When she was parched and exhausted and had lost all hope of rescue, two great owls swam up out of the water, high into the air, swooped down and flew beneath her arms so that their heads formed new breasts for her and their great spans of wings lifted her from behind. She did not look like an angel as she lifted, for her wings were dark and feathery, but she was most certainly holy.

And then the owls held her above the water, suspended, and from the river-sea, eight bluebirds ascended, flew high into the air, looped down and flew between her fingers, lodging their bright heads at the place where fingers became hands.

The woman was weak, but the birds were not. The owls beat their strong wings, the bluebirds joined in the effort, and they carried the woman across the sky, off into the woods.

I turned to look in her direction, and I saw the path to my sacred place, lined with spirits from the river and the air.

I did not know what to worship, and so I worshipped it all. What else could I do?

When Wallace woke up, I told him that I needed to go off on my own. He wanted to come with me, but I refused.

"What if something happens?" he asked.

"Nothing will happen," I told him. "Stay here and fish."

"I thought you wanted to show me the place."

"I do," I assured him, "but not right now. I have to go there first."

"When will you be back?"

"Later today," I promised. "And I need you to be here. Swear that you won't leave."

"I swear," he said, and he took my face, kissed it three times, and said I was a funny creature.

"Suppose I need you," he said. "How can I find you?"

"There's a path through those trees"—I pointed—"I'm going that way. The walk is about fifteen minutes. That's all. But *don't come.*"

"If you aren't back by dusk, I'll look for you," he warned.

"Okay," I said, "but not before."

I dumped everything from my pack except for the dark woman, a knife, and matches, and I made my way to the place in the trees where my private journey began.

Wallace called out, "Be careful."

"You too," I told him, and I stared at him for a moment, looking at his darkness, his age gathered around his eyes, and his light spirit filling him with that glow I'd learned to trust.

"Watch out for snakes," he called again.

"It's under control."

"I'll miss you," he yelled as I walked out of his sight.

"Yeah, right," I called back, smiling to myself as I trudged across the land, breathing easy.

Walking through the woods, I spoke to Mammie for the last time. She was waiting at the river where the three women had camped. I didn't actually see her at all. But looking out over the river at the spot where the women had huddled together in song, I noticed two small stones. With the water running over them, they looked like breasts beneath the surface. The wind blew tiny riplets into the water, wrinkling it, a river's goose pimples. I knew somehow that the aged breasts belonged to Mammie. I could see them breathing in a stone's slight way. Not moving, but no less real.

"Mammie," I called out. "I loved you. I'm sorry."

She heard me. I'm sure of it. For a second, I thought I could see her heart, but it may have been a fish.

It took most of the day to get things ready. I found my own tree, of course, sturdy as ever, the roots dangling down from the ceiling, but I had to clean it out again. Some animal had hidden nuts in the deep crevice, and the damp, dead leaves that had collected inside had to be raked away.

My bone utensils and stone tools still sat outside the tree. I took them to the river where I'd bathed so many times and washed them gently, brought them dripping back to the place where the dark woman waited.

"It feels okay to be here," I told her.

"This was the safest place for you for a while," she said.

I gathered wood and built my fire in the same circle where I'd cooked a year before. Then I threw the small green leaves of water oaks into the fire and listened to them crackle.

"What about your traps? Are they still here?" the dark woman asked.

I hadn't had time to fill them in before I'd left.

Things had happened so quickly. I was glad to have the chance to finish up.

I went to the places where I'd first dug the holes and covered them with layers of ferns and mulch. Some of them had filled in with soil. One contained small bones.

When I returned to the mothering tree, it was already late in the afternoon. The dark woman relaxed on the leaning trunk. I straddled the tree beside her.

"This is the place where I marked up my body," I told her. "Sitting right here."

"What do you need to do—now that you're back in this place?" she asked.

"I don't know."

"Think," she demanded.

I stripped off my clothes, piece by piece, and carried them to the edge of my safe space.

I sought out rocks and balanced them, one on top of the other, carefully and deliberately, until I had built a small altar, a monument of sorts.

"To honor the pain in the world," I told the dark woman.

"Yes," she said.

I stretched out on the tree, felt the bark against my back, the fine mossiness that grew on the bark. I was almost ready. I looked into the sky, into the evening sun, and invoked all the spirits of the women I knew intimately. I had the wax woman with me already, but I called up the mysterious trio I'd met a year earlier. I called up Magdelena from the Laundromat, who had shown me the moon. I even called for St. Agatha, who knew the secret joy of knives through skin.

And, of course, I called the Madonna.

I didn't see them. I didn't need to. They each came separately, cloaking me with their quiet power. I felt them kiss the scarred places on my body. Each one caressed me, whispered me gifts, and then slipped into the dark woman through the hole in her chest.

"I told you it wasn't a flaw," she muttered.

"Yeah, yeah," I said.

Then I cried like a woman, holding back nothing. I cried for the pain of wounds, for the loss of trust, for the joy of getting it all back from the millions of sacred spirits around me, spirits I could breathe. I wailed out, shook, dropped tears so firm they pitted the ground.

It was a twilight celebration. Wallace couldn't miss it.

I heard him shuffling across the earth, calling out, "Jael, is that you?"

"Down here," I laughed. "Come on."

I took his hand and led him to the mothering tree, holding the dark woman and all her kindred spirits beneath my arm.

"Sit down," I said, and pulled him beneath the roots.

I wedged the dark woman into the ground at the tree's doorway, leaned over her, and kissed her scarred chest. Then I struck a match and ignited her mossy hair. As it crinkled, kinked red and sizzled, a thick white light poured into the air. I breathed it deep, sucked in deeper, until nothing was left but smoke.

Wallace reached up, put his hand on my thigh, and pulled me back down beside him. I could feel bits of earth raining over our heads while the dark woman melted at my feet.

She burned like a candle.
I kissed him like a flame.

For as long as I can remember, I've searched for things to worship. I've found gods in crickets and gods reflected in tiny cricket eyes. I've met gods already dead, gods too young to save me. Once I prayed with my palms turned up, ready to receive. That bleak creator spit into my hands.

I've learned to say thank you.

I've learned to mean it.

Gods change colors and spin themselves new garments every day. Sometimes wearing our own aged faces, they tap us on the shoulder, wave to say, "You're going to make it through."

Once a god showed me her faded scar. When I poked it, she said, "Ouch." Then she let me drink her breast milk until dawn.

When you kneel to kiss the god's firm foot, find toes shaped like your own, what can you do besides worship? What can you feel except joy?